DANNY ORLIS
AND THE
GIRL WHO DARED

DANNY ORLIS

AND THE
GIRL WHO
DARED

BERNARD PALMER

Danny Orlis and the Girl Who Dared
© 2024 by Bernard Palmer
All rights reserved. First edition 1974.
Second edition 2024.

Scripture quotations from The Authorized (King James) Version. Rights in the Authorized Version in the United Kingdom are vested in the Crown. Reproduced by permission of the Crown's patentee, Cambridge University Press.

Cover image: Adobe Firefly
Character illustrations: John Ball
Editor: Charlene Miskimen

Aneko Press *Youth*

www.anekopress.com

Aneko Press, Life Sentence Publishing, and our logos are trademarks of Life Sentence Publishing, Inc.
203 E. Birch Street
P.O. Box 652
Abbotsford, WI 54405

JUVENILE FICTION / Religious / Christian / Action & Adventure
Paperback ISBN: 979-8-88936-086-5
eBook ISBN: 979-8-88936-087-2
10 9 8 7 6 5 4 3 2 1
Available where books are sold

CONTENTS

CHAPTER 1

BROTHERS

It was midmorning the day before the new school term was to begin at Rock Point's Northwest High in Colorado. The late summer sun slanted through the family room window in the Warren home to wash the worn carpet with light. DeeDee Davis was sitting on the couch across from the injured Letitia Warren, whose crutches rested against a bookcase within easy reach. She had fallen on a ski run the spring before and badly injured her back. She had only been released from the hospital two weeks before and still found it difficult to get around.

"I'm glad you got out in time for school," DeeDee said. "I was beginning to think you weren't going to make it."

The other girl's thin smile broadened.

"I *knew* God was going to let me start school with the rest of you. I've been praying about it for weeks and weeks." She spoke confidently, as one who had a great deal of experience with answered prayer.

And she had.

From the time she had given her life to Christ, everyone around her saw the power of prayer and the evidence of her new life. The day she left the hospital, nurses who had taken care of her hugged her and made her promise to come back and visit them. She had cried, despite her pleasure at being released. She was going to miss them, especially a young nurse's aide who seemed close to confessing her sin and putting her trust in the Savior. Now Letitia was going back to school, her face bright with excitement and anticipation.

"I can't help wondering who God is going to send my way next," she murmured, "or if that person will pay attention when I share Jesus Christ."

DeeDee watched her friend quietly as the pale sunlight fell onto the crutches by her legs. The change that had come over Letitia in the months since the accident was phenomenal. Before the injury she had been shy and morose most of the time, staggering under a load of inferiority and guilt. Now a new radiance and contentment possessed her.

There seemed to be an inner core of strength she could draw from when discouragement came; a trust that made her sweet and kind, completely at ease, even though she didn't know what the future held for her. Even during those long, pain-racked months in the hospital, she had been cheerful. Her family especially had difficulty in understanding what had happened to her to make her so different. They talked about it often when she was sent home and had to get around the house on crutches.

"I sure don't get it," her brother Hank told DeeDee one day. "Letitia might be stuck on those 'sticks' for life, but I don't think it bothers her. She acts as though it doesn't matter whether she ever is able to walk and run like other kids. Being around her, you get the idea that she doesn't care."

"She cares, all right," DeeDee answered. She had seen the hurt creep into Letitia's luminous eyes at times when the subject came up.

"If she does," Hank said, "she sure doesn't act like it."

"I think Letitia is finding out that God can give a person the strength to get through disappointments. You know, I've experienced that, too, Hank. It's really cool having Jesus on your side."

"You sound just like her, DeeDee," Hank snorted irritably. "And it doesn't hit me any better coming from you than it does from her."

"We're both praying for you."

His cheeks turned crimson, and the color crept down his neck and up to the tips of his ears. "The last thing I need is somebody to pray for me. I'm gettin' along great just as it is!"

He had stormed away then.

DeeDee was thinking about that as she looked over at Letitia. "Did you get to talk to him today?" she wanted to know.

Only then did the smile leave the other girl's sallow face. "I tried, but he wouldn't let me."

"He will," DeeDee replied confidently, not really knowing whether she was as sure of what she said as she would like to be.

"I know." She spoke hesitantly, as though it was suddenly difficult to talk about her brother. "But it's so hard waiting for God to work. I wonder if I ought to get somebody like Bill Anderson to talk to him. Hank's always liked Bill. Now that he's a believer, Hank just might listen to him."

DeeDee nodded.

"Or maybe Del would talk to him if I asked him." She leaned forward intently. "He's your brother. You know him a lot better than I do. Do you think he would?"

"If you asked him," DeeDee said, smiling, "I'm sure he would try."

She didn't want to say anything to cause her friend's discouragement about her brother to increase, but she wasn't at all sure it would do any good to have anyone to talk to him. She had tried it herself, and Hank refused to listen. She didn't think it would be any different if Bill or Del or someone else attempted to share the gospel with him. Right then he didn't act as though he would listen to anyone.

"You'll pray for him, won't you, DeeDee?" Letitia asked.

"You know I will."

* * *

Del and Doug Davis, the other two thirds of the Davis triplets, had talked about going out for the football team at Northwest High that fall but decided against it.

"I wouldn't mind going out if I thought we had half a chance of getting to play," Doug said, "even with the second team. But I'm afraid it's a waste of time."

"That's just the way I feel. Last year we didn't even get to stay on the squad."

Doug kicked a pebble with his toe as they walked along the street toward their house. They were seniors now. This was their last year of eligibility. He'd give a lot to play football again. But there wasn't any use in going out for the team if they were going to be cut from the squad by the end of September.

"I think we'd just as well forget it," Del observed.

"I guess you're right," Doug said, shrugging his own wishes away. "But I'd still like to get another crack at it."

The day school started, however, the coach stopped them in the hall and asked if they were going out for the team.

"We hadn't figured on it," Del told him.

"Come up to my office your first free period," the coach said. "I'd like to talk to you."

Del didn't want to go, but his brother insisted on it.

"What can it hurt?" Doug asked.

"We've already made up our minds what we're going to do, so why talk about it?"

In the end they went to the coach's office, Del still protesting that it couldn't possibly do any good.

The coach was leaning back in his chair when they knocked at the door and entered. He was a huge, well-muscled individual who had played university football. He visited with them for a few minutes, asking what they had been doing that summer and if they thought they were in good shape. Only then did he bring up the subject of playing football.

"We decided against it," Del blurted out.

"You did?" The coach's frown deepened. "What's the matter? Is it too tough for you?"

Doug's cheeks were red. He didn't like the idea of having the coach think they were such weaklings they couldn't take football.

"It's not that," he countered. "We were out for football last year, but both got cut from the squad. We didn't think it would do any good to even go out this year."

"Don't be too sure. The team last year was one of those exceptional outfits that only come along once or twice in a coach's career. And most of the first string were seniors. We lost all but two starters by graduation and one of those moved away last month." He paused. "I can't promise you anything, of course. And I wouldn't if I could. But there are so many positions open I'd say you had a good chance of getting in the starting lineup."

He went on to tell them that they weren't the only ones who were discouraged. A number of guys had decided not to try out that year.

"So, the chances are even better for those who do."

Doug was ready to decide right then, but Del insisted on thinking about it.

"Is it okay if we let you know later?" he asked.

"Don't wait too long. Every day you miss practice is going to make it just that much harder for you to sew up a position."

As soon as they left the coach's office, Del turned to Doug. "I thought we'd already decided we weren't going out for the team this fall."

"That was because we didn't think we'd have a chance. Think of it! We've got a good chance of making the team! I don't see how you can drag your feet!"

Del continued to protest, but he knew from the first that he was beaten. That night he went straight from their final class to the locker room where they checked out their equipment. Now that they were there, the coach seemed indifferent to them. He spoke curtly and turned away.

"See, what'd I tell you?" Del whispered. "He was just giving us a line. He isn't going to give us any better breaks than we got last year. We won't last any longer than the first cut."

Doug frowned him to silence.

It was good to put on a football uniform, Del had to admit, and get out on the field, even though they didn't touch a football at first. The coach had them running around the track and doing strength training. Never far out of shape, the Davis boys were soon moved to one corner of the practice field where they began to practice blocking and tackling. Before the week was out, they were chosen for the first team in the coming scrimmage.

Del still didn't think it meant anything. "Look at the guys who are still trying to get the blubber off and their wind built up. When they're able to play, it'll be different. You'll see that we're moved down pretty quick."

"No, just you wait. We're both going to make it this time."

The first practice game didn't go too badly, in spite of the fact that everybody was tense and a little ragged. Both Davis boys were started on the offensive eleven, but midway in the second quarter Doug was switched from the backfield to the defensive tackle. Bill Anderson was playing tight end, and Hank Warren was in the tailback slot.

The coach did a lot of yelling at them that afternoon and frequently stopped the play to chew out someone for a mistake they would never make later in the season. Still, he seemed to be satisfied with the play and complimented Del on the way he played.

"You did all right out there this afternoon, Davis," he said on the way to the locker room. "Keep up the good work. We're going to need two or three guys like you."

Del glanced in his direction, grinning. He had done his best. Everyone had to agree to that. Maybe being out for football wasn't so bad after all.

CHAPTER 2

A REQUEST FOR PRAYER

Neither Del nor Doug was on the starting lineup when the first game was played, but they got in a lot of time. Doug was still at defensive tackle. He played a steady although unspectacular game, making four or five tackles and stripping away the blockers on two other plays so the end could smear the ball carrier for no gain. Del, however, distinguished himself with a touchdown and two long runs.

When the game was over, Doug went over to him. "That was great! I was sure proud of you out there tonight."

Del grinned. A couple of the other guys had congratulated him, too, but what they said hadn't meant nearly as much as that brief word from Doug. His brother wasn't jealous of him at all. He was really glad that Del had done so well on the football field. That made it mean all the more to him.

"You were okay out there, too," he answered. "I heard the coach say we don't have anyone else who can hit half as hard as you do."

"We'll keep smearing up the opposition if you'll get a few points for us every game. Okay?"

"It's a deal!"

Del felt great as he showered and dressed. Doug was the finest brother any guy could ever have.

Bill Anderson came over to them as they were leaving the school building. "You guys played a good game tonight."

"You did all right yourself," Del replied.

"Well, we won, so I guess that proves we all did some things right." He offered them a ride home. "I've got something I'd like to talk with you about."

"Sorry," Doug said, "but I've got a date."

"Little Miss Cadillac can get along without you for a little while, can't she?"

"Oh no," Del broke in. "Doug doesn't keep *her* waiting. She might not like it if he did."

"Okay, wise guys! Wrap it up!"

"You go ahead, Doug. I'll fill you in tonight when you get home."

Doug Davis turned. "It's going to be a relief to get away from you guys."

They were still laughing as he joined Tina Nicholson and disappeared into the darkness.

"What was so funny back there?" she asked him.

He was glad for the darkness to hide the red in

his cheeks. "It's just a little private joke those two characters cooked up."

Bill and Del climbed into Bill's car. Bill put the key into the ignition and revved the motor. He turned to Del. "I saw Letitia Warren at noon today. She wants me to talk to Hank about his need of Jesus Christ."

Del waited uncomfortably. He hoped Bill wasn't going to ask him to talk with Hank. About all he could do with Hank would be to make him so mad he'd lose a friend. He wasn't the kind of guy who'd listen to the gospel.

Still, Del felt compelled to offer to help. "Is there anything I can do?" he asked reluctantly.

"I thought maybe you and Doug would pray for me. I don't know much about sharing Christ. It's hard for me to explain things. I understand my new beliefs and yet I don't know how I can make them real to Hank."

Del was quick to assure Bill that they would pray for him and Hank every day. He was thankful they were being asked to do something like praying. It was important, there was no doubt of that. It was safe, too. He could pray for Bill and Hank, and no one would ever know anything about it. He wouldn't be risking Hank's loss as a friend.

The Davis boys kept their word about praying for the other two boys. Once or twice Del felt like asking Bill how things were going – if he had been able to talk to Hank yet about his need to put his trust in Jesus Christ. He decided against it, however. Even casual talk could get him involved more than he wanted to be.

* * *

Del and Doug were so busy with their studies and football that they had heard nothing about the new missionary family that had moved to Rock Point during the summer. They were sitting at the supper table after finishing their meal when Danny Orlis mentioned the Trumbo family and the fact that they would be living in town for a year.

"Virgil is taking our flying course," Danny explained. "I guess he'll be flying for his mission when he goes back out to the field."

"Do they have any girls?" Doug asked.

His brother laughed. "What do you care? You've already got Tina."

"So I was just asking."

"As a matter of fact," inserted Danny," they do have a daughter, but she's a little young for either of you. In fact, they've got two kids in the family – a girl and a boy."

Del glanced knowingly at his sister. She stiffened, knowing what to expect from him.

"Oh, so that's what's been putting the bloom in the cheeks of our loving sister," he said.

"No," she retorted defensively. "The fact that

this Trumbo family has a son hasn't done a thing for me. If you really want to know what I've been doing, you can ask Letitia. I've been spending most of my time with her." DeeDee's eyes danced. "I had to protect your interests there by spending so much time with her she wouldn't look for somebody else to take *your* place."

She continued. "Besides, for your information, Gary Trumbo happens to be all of twelve or thirteen years old. He's just a bit young for me."

"That would be all right," Del said. "You could train him just the way you want him." Triumphantly, he scooped the last few cake crumbs from his plate into a spoon and ate them.

DeeDee studied the tablecloth. "Actually, if Gary were a little older, I just might be interested. Is he ever handsome! He's already got the build of a football player! I can imagine what he's going to look like when he gets a little older."

"Why wouldn't he look like a football player?" Danny put in. "His dad was All-American at Alabama."

The boys stared doubtfully at him.

"You've got to be kidding about this Virgil Trumbo," Doug said. "A missionary who was All-American?"

"As a matter of fact, I'm not kidding." Danny poured himself another cup of coffee. "Virge not only was All-American in his university days, he played pro football for several years before he was converted and felt the call to fulltime missionary service."

Del was interested in the missionary who was on furlough in Rock Point, but not half so much as his brother. Doug had dozens of questions for Danny. He followed Danny into the living room.

"What team was he with?" he asked. "What position did he play? How many years was he a pro?"

At last Danny threw up his arms in a wide gesture to stem the flood of questions. "Now wait a minute, Doug. I've only known Virge for a month or so. I wouldn't have a clue about most of the things you've asked me. If you want to get the answers to all of those questions, you'll have to talk to him yourself. That's all I can tell you."

"I figure on doing that the first chance I get." He breathed deeply. "Do you suppose he'd come out to the field some time when he isn't too busy and give us some pointers? A guy like him could help us a lot."

Danny thought a moment. "I wouldn't know about that. He's taking courses in the ground school as well as flight instruction. Also he works in a store in one of the shopping centers. Plus he's got a family to spend time with. He wouldn't have a lot of time to come and show anyone anything about playing football. Still, it wouldn't hurt to ask him."

Doug and Del decided they ought to talk with the coach first. The next afternoon they spoke with him before practice.

"I've been hearing about him, but I haven't had a chance to meet him yet," the coach said. "Why don't you guys bring him around some time? I think we'd all like to hear what he could tell us about playing football."

Doug promised that they would just as soon as he had a free afternoon. When they were out on the practice field a few minutes later, Del turned to him. "And how do you plan on bringing Mr. Trumbo out here to see the coach and talk with the guys? We don't even know the man, and here you are arranging meetings for him. Why don't you book the President for a speech too?"

Doug grinned. "I haven't quite figured it out yet. I thought maybe you'd go and talk to him."

"Fat chance. I didn't make any promises. This is your little project now."

"Maybe we can get Danny to talk to Mr. Trumbo," suggested Doug.

"Well, you'd better get to work on it. If you can't get him here," Del added, "we're both going to be in a jam."

Doug talked with Danny about asking Mr. Trumbo to come out to the school and talk to the guys about football, but he refused. "You've got a tongue, Doug. You can ask him yourself. Tell you what, though, I'll introduce you to him."

The boys hoped to get to meet Virgil Trumbo within the next two or three days. Although Del teased Doug a lot about the trouble he was building for himself, he was as anxious to meet the professional football player as Doug was. At first Danny was too busy to take them over and make the introductions, then when Danny had free time, Virgil Trumbo had to work or study.

* * *

Letitia Warren was able to start school on time, but there were days when she had to put aside her crutches for a wheelchair, which DeeDee or one of the other kids wheeled from one class to another. The first day she saw Del at school, her face brightened, and she moved her chair toward him, pushing on the wheels with her hands.

"Hi, Del."

"Hi."

They fell silent.

He didn't know why it bothered him so much to talk to her. She was the same as any of DeeDee's other friends, and he could joke with them and tease them as easily as he did his sister. Only it wasn't quite true that she was the same as DeeDee's other friends. She was different than the others – a lot different.

He stammered slightly as he asked her how things had been going for her since she got out of the hospital. Her self-consciousness and embarrassment were gone, and she talked to him very naturally.

"Oh, I have so many things to tell you that I don't even know where to begin." In her excitement the words tumbled out, one over the other. "The Lord has worked in my life in such a wonderful way this past summer that there are times when I have to pinch myself to see whether or not I'm dreaming."

Del nodded. He had heard in letters from DeeDee the past three months that Letitia's spiritual growth had been significant.

"I've had the most tremendous summer of my life!" she exclaimed.

He studied her face seriously. She didn't even have to tell him that. Nor would he have had to depend on what DeeDee wrote. Just looking at her was enough to let him see that everything about her was different.

"I'm anxious to hear about it," he said. At that moment the bell sounded. "I've got to run, Letitia."

But before he left, he made a date to have lunch with her at noon. "I'll meet you in the hall outside the cafeteria. I want to hear all about your summer."

"And I want to hear what you and Doug did too."

She was weaker than she realized and found herself tiring easily in spite of her wheelchair. She was glad she hadn't done as she wanted to and come to school on crutches that morning. She could get around well enough on crutches, but it was so much more tiring than the wheelchair. Still, wheelchair or not, it was good to be back in school.

Letitia had been praying all summer about the time when she could go back to classes with the rest of the kids. She had already decided it would be an opportunity to tell them what God had done for her. She had talked with many of those who came up to the hospital to see her. But there were so many in school who only knew her so casually they wouldn't have even thought about visiting her in the hospital.

Kids like that wouldn't have known anything about the change that came into her life. Most of them wouldn't know anything about Jesus Christ or the fact that He died on the cross and was raised again so they could have a triumphant, happy life for now and eternity.

The first few days at school she was tense and more than a little apprehensive. What if she couldn't keep up with the schedule? What if the kids avoided her because of her injury? Or worse, what if they showered her with pity? That would be hard to take, too.

One of the girls who sat across the aisle from her in the study hall eyed her curiously. "I couldn't help hearing you tell Del Davis that you'd had the most wonderful summer you've ever had," she said, doubt creeping into her voice. "You must have been joking."

"Oh, no." Letitia's smile beamed warmly at her. "I really meant it. It's been a tremendous summer."

The other girl could not believe her. "You were in the hospital, and most of the time you were in a cast so you couldn't even move," she went on, eyeing the brace Letitia still wore. "And you still aren't able to do a lot of the things the rest of us do. I don't see how you could say you had such a great vacation."

"But it was," the Warren girl protested. "And I'm going to have a good time in school this year, too, even if I'm not able to do a lot with the rest of my friends. It's all in God's hands. If He doesn't want me to take part in the activities here at school, He'll give me something else to do."

The other girl had known Letitia for almost two years but could never remember having seen her truly happy – that is, until now.

The rest of the afternoon she found herself thinking about her slender friend. Seeing Letitia so radiantly happy made her feel she was missing out on a great deal. She had her health and everything that Letitia didn't have right then – and may never have. She could go to parties and football games and out on dates. She thought she was having a ball. But she realized that she didn't have the radiance and peace the other girl had. She couldn't understand it.

CHAPTER 3

THE ENGLISH THEME

The second football game of the season was tougher than anyone thought it had a right to be. Northwest was playing Lander, a small-town team that was supposed to be a pushover for the big school. They had lost their first two encounters that season and had dropped their last four games to the Rock Point high school. Even Del and Doug found themselves looking beyond the Lander team to the game the following Friday night, which was with an opponent much more worthy of Northwest's attention.

Only the coach seemed concerned about the outcome of the Lander game. "You guys are all taking this game too lightly," he informed them caustically. "You're either not as good as you think you are, or Lander is a lot better than you give it credit for being."

The guys on the football squad cringed under the withering attack.

"If you don't go in there and give us your best, you're going to get skinned. And if it happens, you'll deserve it."

Mentally, Del promised himself that he was going to knock out a couple of TD's for the coach, just to show him he didn't know what he was talking about.

Shortly after the opening kickoff, however, he learned that Lander was a much stronger team than he had expected. They were up, too, determined to give Northwest a battle for every touchdown.

Seconds after the first quarter opened, the smaller school recovered a fumble on the Northwest twenty-eight-yard line. In six sharply executed plays, they punched across the goal to forge ahead by six points. The kick was successful, increasing the lead to 7-0.

The rest of the first half was scoreless, and so was the third quarter. As the fourth quarter opened, Northwest got on the scoreboard with a long field goal no one expected them to make, cutting the Lander lead by four points to 7-3.

The kickoff was an onside kick, and Northwest recovered. On the next play, a deceptive fake to the fullback with Del carrying, he was able to scoot past the linebacker and into the open. With a terrific burst of speed he flew along the sidelines. A roar went up from the crowd. He was sure he was going all the way. And then, on the nine-yard line, a tackler came roaring in out of nowhere to nail him!

A roar went up from the stands as Del took his

position in the backfield once more. Everyone, including the Lander defensive unit, thought he would be carrying the ball again. But the quarterback only faked the ball to the fleet-footed Davis boy. He kept it himself and swept around right end, gathering momentum before the defensive unit realized what was happening. They nailed him, but not until he had gained four yards.

That gave the powerful fullback, Dick Majors, the incentive he needed to dive over the center to the three-and-a-half-yard line. While Lander was still reeling, Dick sped across for the TD that gave Northwest the lead.

Lander came snarling back, valiantly, but this time Doug and his companions on the defensive line refused to yield. Lander was forced to punt on the fourth down.

The smaller school continued to play well defensively, and on occasion they were able to make a little ground through the Northwest line, but they could not put a sustained drive together. Two or three short runs, and Northwest would stiffen to hold them to downs, so they would be forced to punt. They made a few first downs, but when the yardage really counted, the stubborn Northwest defensive refused to yield.

After that brief flurry of scoring, neither team could put a sustained drive together. The scoring for the evening was over. But for Northwest that really didn't matter. They had managed to pull out a victory when it looked as though they were about to lose.

Doug hurried to walk back to the locker room with his brother after the game was over.

"You sure pulled this one out for us, Del," he said. "We'd have been wiped out if it hadn't been for you and that long run."

Del didn't agree. "I just happened to be lucky, that's all. The line opened holes for me. That's the only way I was able to do anything."

Once they were in the locker room, the coach came over and congratulated him. "We almost got what we deserved tonight, Davis. If it hadn't been for you, we'd have been whipped badly. If you keep up that kind of play, you're going to be in our starting lineup. How does that grab you?"

Del thanked him and sat down on a nearby bench to untie his shoes. The victory and the things the coach had said didn't mean as much to him as he would have expected. He was glad to know the coach thought he played a good game, but it really didn't set him up.

Just a year ago he had really been upset because he hadn't been able to make the squad. Now he had set up the winning touchdown, and he didn't feel that surge of elation he expected would be his. He still enjoyed playing, and he was glad he had survived the first and second cuts and could get in some playing time. It wouldn't have been the truth to deny that. Yet it was just a game.

Doug wouldn't be able to understand such an attitude. He had a fierce competitive spirit that didn't seem to be able to take defeat. And that was something Del just didn't have. Winning or losing didn't mean all that much to him.

The following week the coach shook up both the offensive and defensive units after a scathing lecture that ripped down most of the guys.

"It's a good thing we were playing a team like Landers last Friday night," he said. "If we'd been playing someone who was really tough, we'd have had it."

Some of the guys who had been starters the first two games were demoted to the second squad, and others who had had little chance to play found themselves with the first string. Del was used more in scrimmage than he had been since the season began.

The coach had Cliff Henderson, the quarterback, run some new plays designed specifically for Del and indicated that he was going to be depending on him for much of the team's scoring punch.

"Some of you may wonder why I'm using Davis so much," he announced, "but I like his aggressiveness and the way he kept boring in after Lander got the jump on us and scored."

Del squirmed uncomfortably. He wanted to tell the coach that he hoped he didn't disappoint him.

"Davis gives us everything he's got every minute

he's on the field," the coach continued. "That's why I'm going to use him in our next game or two. If any of the rest of you get any ideas about beating him out of his position, there's only one way you can do it. That is to play better football than Del does."

Doug, however, got to play only a few minutes each game. He thought it would help him get in more playing time when he was moved to the defensive unit, but it didn't seem to make much difference. He was put in when the coach wanted to tell the other tackle something or if the first-string guy was shaken up. Otherwise Doug sat on the bench until the dying moments of the game. Then he would be shoved in, playing when the game was already won or lost.

He didn't like that much, but he didn't complain about it. Tina was the one who spoke about it.

"I don't think it's fair that you only get to play such a short time each game," she said. "I don't think it's fair at all, and I don't see why you put up with it."

"Don't let yourself get so upset about it," he said. "It's my own fault."

"I don't see how you can say that," she retorted.

He laughed. "If I could play better, I'd be out there more, Tina. It's as simple as that."

"I don't know how you can say that, Doug," she countered. "You're as good as anyone on the defensive team. When you're in there, who makes the tackles? You do."

"The trouble is I don't make enough of them."

"It isn't fair."

Doug changed the subject.

In the next game Del alternated at running back, getting to play almost half the time and doing an excellent job. He didn't make any spectacular runs, but could be counted on for consistent ground gaining. When he came off the field for the last time, the coach thumped him approvingly on the back. "You were good out there again tonight, Davis. We're all proud of you."

He glanced at the coach and grinned.

* * *

Letitia Warren had continued to pray about her classmates, asking God to help her take advantage of the opportunities that came her way to witness to them. She discussed it with DeeDee on several occasions.

"When I'm with the kids," she said, "I want to tell them about Jesus Christ so bad that I ache inside for them."

DeeDee nodded understandingly. She was concerned about the kids at school, too. She prayed for them often. But she had to admit that she didn't even come close to having the concern for her friends and schoolmates that Letitia had.

DeeDee had been given an assignment to write a theme for English, but she hadn't even considered it as an opportunity to share Jesus Christ with the other kids in the room. She was as surprised as anyone in the class when the teacher asked Letitia to read her theme and she learned what her friend had written.

Letitia hadn't brought her wheelchair to school that day, so she stood beside her desk, leaning on her crutches to read the paper she had written. Her hands were shaking so much she could scarcely hold the theme, and her cheeks were dark with embarrassment. But when she finally began to read, her voice was clear and firm.

"It may sound strange when I write that I am glad I broke my back and had to spend so many months in the hospital. But I am. I am glad for every hour of pain – for every minute of disappointment and frustration.

"For those are the things God used to cause me to see my need to turn my life completely and totally to Jesus Christ. Because of what happened to me, I realized that I had to commit my life to Him."

As she continued, the teenagers in the class were struck silent, stunned by the message of her theme. When she finally reached the end, a hush settled over the group of kids in the room. One of her girlfriends was crying softly. Some were staring fixedly at Letitia, as though she was some strange individual they had never seen before. Others looked at the floor, the ceiling, the walls. She started to ease back into her seat, but stopped and spoke again, as earnestly as before.

"I *know* that some of you are probably thinking

I've exaggerated when I wrote as I did about being glad that I fell on the ski slope and broke my back. But I'm telling you the truth. If I hadn't been hurt and spent those weeks in the hospital, I wouldn't have taken a long, hard look at myself. And I wouldn't have known the thrill I have now. I would still be wallowing so deep in self-pity that I wouldn't have any room for Jesus Christ. I would still be living a defeated life." She stopped abruptly, embarrassed by her own outspokenness.

"Thank you, Letitia," the teacher said quietly. "Thank you very much."

CHAPTER 4

DEEDEE APOLOGIZES

In the hush that followed Letitia's theme, the instructor crossed the room reflectively and stood at the window for a time, only half mindful of the waiting class. Then, remembering where she was and what she was doing, she came back to her desk and asked one of the boys to read what he had written.

He went to the front of the room and began to read, almost apologetically, as though it wasn't quite right for him to break the atmosphere created by Letitia's theme. He was on the staff of the student paper, and his work was always good, but most of the kids scarcely paid attention. They were still thinking about Letitia's account of her experience in the hospital and what she had said at the end.

The teacher too, was caught up by the mood of the injured girl's composition. She went to church with some degree of regularity and always had considered herself as a religious person. But she had never had anything that could be compared with Letitia's experience. It made her wonder if her faith really amounted to anything.

She became aware of the fact that the boy had finished reading and was about to sit down.

"Just a minute, James," she said. "Can you tell us the main thrust of your theme?"

He studied her face questioningly. "It's in the title, Miss Martin. 'The Effect of Ecology on Modern Life.'"

"Oh, yes," she said hastily, embarrassed by her own inattentiveness.

She asked a few general questions of the class about the paper, complimented him on it, and asked for another composition to be read. No one was really listening.

When it was finally over, Miss Martin wanted to go and talk with Letitia, but several of the girls had already crowded around her. Reluctantly the teacher went back and sat down.

"That was wonderful, Letitia," one of the girls said. "I don't believe I've ever heard anything that touched me the way your theme did this afternoon."

Another girl spoke up. "Oh, I'd give anything to be able to write the way you do."

She thanked them for the kind things they said and picked up her books, dropping them into a shoulder bag that left her arms free for her crutches. She was deeply disappointed. She had been planning such big things for her theme. She first decided to write it because it would be a way of getting her testimony before the kids. All the while she wrote, she had prayed that God would give her exactly the right words to challenge the people in the room. She had been so excited about her theme that she had been able to think of little else all day.

Now she had read it, and nothing happened. The only ones who seemed to be deeply impressed were those who were taken up with the skill she had been able to employ in writing it. A few months before that would have meant a great deal to her. Today it was incidental to her real hopes.

Letitia started slowly for the door on her crutches, struggling to keep back the tears that threatened to rush down her cheeks at any moment. She was out in the hall when Audrey Burton came up to her. Audrey didn't live too far from the church, but she never went. She was a dark-haired, rebellious senior who ran with a rough crowd. Whenever Letitia had talked with her, she boasted about the weed parties and beer bashes she had been to. The girls didn't know whether she really did all the things she kept bragging about or not, but she certainly wasn't interested in Christian things.

"Did you want to talk to me?" Letitia asked curiously as they moved down the hall together.

"I just want to ask you a couple of questions. Do

you really believe that stuff you read in your theme this afternoon?" Audrey demanded belligerently.

Letitia moved closer to the wall where she could stop without running the risk of being knocked down and turned to face her companion. "I certainly do," she said, struggling to keep calm. She always felt on the defensive when she talked with Audrey. Even now she had to fight against it. But the fact that she was disturbed was not apparent in her voice. "I believe every single word of it."

"You can't be serious! You just got out of your wheelchair last week and you're wearing a brace and are on crutches now." She shook her head in doubt. "I can't believe it, Letitia. You've got to be feeding us a line. You can't mean it when you say you're so happy."

The Christian girl smiled. "I keep doubting it myself, Audrey. At times I wonder if I'm really me because I'm not built that way. You know how I used to be. Always feeling sorry for myself. I kept myself miserable thinking I could never do anything right. But Jesus Christ came into my life. He is the one who has made me happy. I couldn't be happy in my own strength. If I had to depend on myself, I don't think I could stand to face even one day on these crutches."

A strange wistfulness crept into the other girl's eyes and a longing in her hard young face. She reached out with trembling fingers to touch Letitia's sleeve. "I used to think you were a loser, but I'd give *anything* to have a faith like that, to really have something to believe in."

With that she was gone, hurrying up the hall to her next class.

Letitia stared after her, thanksgiving welling in her heart. God had answered her prayer after all. He hadn't touched the entire class as she had been praying. At least she hadn't seen any visible results of that, but He had worked in Audrey's heart.

As soon as school was out for the day she went to her locker where she was to meet DeeDee. She could scarcely wait to tell her friend what had happened. They waited until the big rush of kids was gone before making their way out to the front steps where Mrs. Warren was to pick them up.

"How did the theme go?" DeeDee asked curiously.

"I've got to tell you!" She shared the entire class period with her friend, ending with the story of Audrey Burton. "Isn't that tremendous?"

DeeDee nodded. Audrey was just about the last person she would ever expect to be interested in spiritual things. She was so tough that few of the boys had any respect for her.

"I'll have to talk with Audrey again," Letitia continued. "But I haven't been able to figure out how I can do it without making it seem contrived and pointed. Do you think I could call her and ask her to come over so I can witness to her again?"

DeeDee thought for a moment. "I don't know. She's

really a tough customer. She might resent it if you did something so obvious. But there must be other times here at school when you can get to know her better. Aren't you in several classes with her? Maybe you could sit next to her in class."

Letitia was enthusiastic about that suggestion. "Audrey always sits in the back of the class by herself. You know, DeeDee, I think maybe she's lonely. Maybe that's why she does all the wild things she brags about. She really needs somebody to be nice to her."

DeeDee said goodbye to Letitia and walked out into the fall sunshine. Letitia's concern for Audrey made DeeDee feel like a hard, insensitive person.

I do care about the other kids, DeeDee said to herself. *And I want to see them find Jesus Christ so that God can control their lives. But all I do is just pray for them now and then. When have I ever shown real friendliness and concern for somebody like Audrey? Mostly I feel superior to her kind. Why, I'm just like one of those old Pharisees! "Thank you, God, that I'm not like the kids who don't go to church." DeeDee, you're a real hypocrite!*

That night she twisted and turned restlessly in bed, staring up at the ceiling. Her Christian life seemed empty and meaningless. She had to have the same joy and excitement about the Lord that Letitia had.

She got out of bed and went over to the window, where she stared out into the darkness. *Life won't be worth living,* she thought, *unless I have more reality in my Christian life. I must have more concern for others.*

Tears were streaming down her cheeks as she went back and knelt beside her bed. She began to pray silently.

"Dear God, I want the peace Letitia has and her concern for the kids around her, that they might come to You. And I want her boldness to show what You have done for me with those who don't know You or even care about You. I want it more than anything else in all the world."

She continued to talk to God, asking His help and guidance.

"And if I have hurt anyone, or if I've done anything wrong that I can correct, help me to know about it so I can go to them and ask for forgiveness."

When at last she finished praying, she felt little different than before. At first she wondered whether anything had happened. It didn't seem that there was anything different in her life.

Then she remembered a teacher she had been talking about the week before. She hadn't said anything terribly bad about her, but she had been upset because the teacher had given a test that didn't seem to be fair, and she was angry enough to repeat some things she had heard. What she said had been unkind. She realized she would have to go to the person she told the unkind things to and make things right.

Then there were Del and Doug. They were only

her brothers, so she thought at first that what she said to them didn't count. But the more she considered it, the more she knew that she had to make things right with them too.

She had been so mad at them so many times she couldn't begin to remember. And when that happened she said some terrible things to them. When she was younger, she used to kick them in the shins. That had stopped, but she supposed talking to them the way she did now was even worse.

They weren't always so nice to her either. That was her first excuse. She soon realized, however, that that was their problem. What they did about getting things straightened out with her was not her concern. She had to get her own life on the right track.

The more she went over the past few months in her mind, the more she became aware that she had wronged others as well. She would have to go to them and ask for their forgiveness.

A few weeks ago – even a few hours ago, she would have resisted any such actions passionately, finding all sorts of excuses for getting out of it. Now, however, she was determined to get with it, to wipe the slate clean so she could have the peace and joy she longed for so much.

The following morning Del and Doug were already at the kitchen table when she came into the room. Danny and Kay were there, as well.

"You're up early this morning, DeeDee," Danny said.

Del noted the serious look on her face. "And she's just as sunny and cheerful as ever."

DeeDee was so intent she was only dimly aware of what they were saying. She looked around uneasily, not knowing whether to talk in front of Danny and Kay or not.

"You'd better break out the castor oil, Kay," Doug put in. "From the look on DeeDee's face, she's been eating too many green apples again."

"Or maybe she lost a new boyfriend we don't know anything about," Del said.

"Is there something wrong, DeeDee?" Kay wanted to know.

"I–I've got something I have to talk with Del and Doug about."

By this time they were all aware that she was serious.

"We've finished breakfast, DeeDee," Danny said, pushing back from the table. "Do you want Kay and me to leave?"

"Oh, no," she answered quickly. That really wasn't true. She did want them to leave. What she was about to do would be hard enough with just Del and Doug there. It would be even worse having Danny and Kay present. But she knew she couldn't ask them to go. "I mean, I've got to talk to the boys in front of you."

"What's this all about?" Del demanded curiously. "It can't be that big a deal!"

DeeDee took a deep breath and began.

"I've been mad at Del and Doug and ripped into them in front of you and Kay. I guess it's no more than right that I ask their forgiveness in front of you."

Del's eyes widened.

"Forgiveness?" Incredulity crept into Doug's voice. "Now I know you are sick, DeeDee." He glanced at Kay. "You'd better get a double dose of *something* for her. She's got to be sick to admit she has ever done anything wrong when it comes to Del and me."

And that's exactly the kind of comment that makes me mad, thought DeeDee. *Lord, please give me self-control so I can get through this.* She told them she realized how unkind she had been to them, how she had lost her temper and said all sorts of things to them that she shouldn't have said.

"I knew I shouldn't do it, even while I was saying those things. I just wanted to hurt you. Will you forgive me?"

For the first time they realized that she really was concerned and meant the things she was saying. Doug and Del glanced at each other quickly.

"DeeDee," Del told her. "You aren't the one who should be asking for forgiveness. Doug and I are the guys who need it. We've given you a terrible time."

"That's right. We've teased you so much we've made you cry and then made fun of you for crying.

We've deserved everything you've said to us. No wonder you fly back at us. I sure do forgive you. No question about that. Will you forgive *me*?"

"Yeah, and me too," Del put in.

DeeDee was stunned. Never had she expected *this* response from her brothers.

At the breakfast table that morning, the five of them had a time of prayer and thanksgiving that was different, somehow, from any other prayer time they had had in recent months. When they finished, Kay went over and kissed DeeDee impulsively.

"I am so happy about this, DeeDee. That took a lot of courage to do."

Danny smiled and nodded.

However, Del had difficulty realizing what was happening.

"I sure don't get it. First of all Letitia Warren changes so much no one would know her. She's the happiest kid in school when she's got every reason to be downhearted and feeling sorry for herself. And she's always talking to someone at school about what God has done for her. The rest of us *talk* about shar-ing. She does it."

He gestured expressively. "Now DeeDee comes through with this! It makes me wonder what kind of a Christian life I'm living anyway."

"Want me to tell you?" Doug broke in. "You're living the same kind I am, and it isn't much. At least it isn't anything when we compare it to what the girls have."

Del did not reply. He was tempted to go after the same thing Letitia and DeeDee had. Only they didn't know too much about what had happened to their sister yet. Maybe it wouldn't last.

When the triplets left the table some minutes later, there was a new relationship among them. DeeDee felt clean and happy inside. Doug whistled as he gathered up his books.

As DeeDee went to the closet for her coat, she decided she had already taken the big step. She had asked God to help her and had started by asking Del and Doug's forgiveness. He would give her strength to continue.

CHAPTER 5

DOUG KEEPS CALM

Letitia Warren was already at her desk when DeeDee entered their homeroom that morning. She had thought she would wait until they had lunch together at noon before telling her friend what had happened. But, seeing Letitia, she got so excited she had to tell her. She hurried over to her friend.

"I've been a Christian for a long time," she said, "but all these years I've been living as though Jesus Christ didn't actually mean anything to me."

"DeeDee, that's not true!" protested Letitia. "Seeing the way you live was the first thing God used to touch my own heart. I knew that I didn't have what you have, and I wanted it desperately."

"Maybe I did exaggerate a little," DeeDee laughed. "I *have* wanted to serve Jesus. But it's true that I have been going through the form of worshiping Him. I haven't been real for some time now. And seeing you and the change that has come over you the last few months has made me realize how much I've been missing. When I heard you talking about Audrey yesterday afternoon, I realized that I need to care more about the people around me. I want to be as happy and as effective for Jesus Christ as you are." She went on to tell Letitia that she had started by getting things right with Del and Doug and that she was going to see a couple of her girlfriends. "I can't go on being 'half a Christian.' I'm turning everything in my life over to Him."

Tears flooded Letitia's eyes. She wiped them away. "Oh, DeeDee!" she exclaimed. "You don't know how that makes me feel. I don't deserve the things you've been saying, but if I've been able to help you even a little bit, it makes me very happy!"

DeeDee hadn't thought about the sort of reaction Letitia would have. She had been so excited she had been able to think only of telling her about it. She certainly hadn't figured there would be tears. But now they shared the happiness of the moment with tears streaming down their faces. Because they both had arrived at school early, the empty classroom gave them privacy.

"I know we've got to follow Jesus and not other Christians," DeeDee said, wiping her eyes with a tissue, "but you've inspired me to make a complete surrender of my life to Him. I wouldn't have realized that I had any need in my life. I'd have gone on the way I have been, trying to live on the strength of the church and Danny and Kay and not growing at all."

Letitia could not speak. She reached over and took DeeDee's hand tenderly. She was glad that her best friend had found encouragement in what she saw in her life. It made her feel as though she had accomplished something after all, that living a Christian life was worthwhile.

There was still Hank, who gave no indication he would ever turn to Jesus. More than once she had almost given up on him. But this was enough to give her faith that God would one day bring her brother to Himself. Quietly she prayed for him.

* * *

During the next two or three football games, Del suddenly seemed to find himself, playing with a sureness and skill that astonished everyone, including the coaching staff. He had been confident enough of his ability at Fairview, and when he and Doug tried out for the team the year before, there had been no doubt in his mind that they would both make it. When neither he nor his brother could even stay on the squad at Northwest last season, he had been badly shaken. So this year Del had been sure the roof would fall in and they would find themselves on the outside once more.

That did not happen, however.

Del soon established himself as one of the top ball carriers on the offensive team. He was able to unravel some important runs at times when they counted the most and had been consistent in his ground gaining whenever he got his hands on the ball. He didn't score a single touchdown during the first part of the season, but he set up the winning score in one game and helped add a little insurance in another by taking a quick lateral from the quarterback as he was about to be tackled, plunging forward another nine yards to put the ball within field goal range. Their kicker came on and booted the ball between the uprights to put three more points on the board.

Del got to start only part of the time, but that didn't particularly bother him. He played at least half the time, and he knew who they called on when the going was tough. His confidence came slowly, but it came. He was calm and completely at ease, regardless of the score or the time left on the board. Before the season was half over, he had won his letter, while Doug was still struggling to get in enough time to earn his.

Doug didn't particularly like playing defense, but he kept plugging away unspectacularly. He made his share of tackles and was adept at smearing the blockers so someone else could get to the guy with the ball. The trouble was that Northwest had two other men for his position. One was a little better than Doug. So he kept slugging away as best he could, grateful for any time he got to put in.

Tina was much more upset by this situation than Doug was. She complained frequently to him about it.

"I can't understand it, Doug," she told him. "Del gets to play so much, and the coach doesn't use you half as much. You're every bit as good as he is."

"That's not what counts," he said, laughing good-naturedly. "Del's practically at the top of the heap when it comes to backs, and I'm trying to beat out a guy who can play circles around me. That's the reason I'm holding down the bench while Del's out there carrying the ball."

"The coach could use you on offense if he wanted to. There's nothing that says you *have* to be defensive tackle."

"Don't knock it, Tina. I didn't even make the squad last year."

"But you're as good as Del is. Everybody says so."

"Everybody except the coach and his assistant, and they're long on Del right now."

"You ought to go in and talk to the coach about it. You could let him know that he's discriminating against you."

Doug didn't agree with her. "Nothing doing. If I went and talked to him, I'd be asked to turn in my uniform. There's only one way a guy can get to play for Northwest. That's by doing a better job than anybody else. It's as simple as that."

"But it isn't!" She was so upset she was close to tears. "It isn't fair at all."

Doug paused and pulled in a deep breath. It would be easy for Tina to get him to feel sorry for himself. There had been a time before they left Fairview when he and Del had scarcely spoken to each other because of jealousy over playing football. He could slip into that same ugly hole again if he allowed himself to think much about it. He had to put a stop to it.

"You know, Tina," he said quietly, "if it's all the same to you, I'd just as soon that we talk about something else."

Hurt gleamed in her eyes. "I'm sorry, Doug. I was just telling you how I feel about the way you're being treated."

"You didn't do anything you shouldn't. It's just that I'm afraid I will if I don't get to thinking about something else."

She waited for him to continue.

"I hadn't figured on telling you this, but I guess I'd better explain it all to you, so you'll know what the pitch is."

"I think you should."

He explained to her how things had been back in Fairview between him and Del because they both played football and how much trouble they had getting things worked out between them, so there was no more jealousy and hard feelings.

"I like to play football," he went on, "and I sure would like to be in the starting lineup now and get to play a lot more. Football's my favorite sport, and

I think I want to get in there and play as much as any other guy on the squad. But I can tell you from what happened back in Fairview that getting to play isn't worth having any trouble between Del and me."

He shifted his books from one arm to the other. "I've finally reached the place where I'm real happy that Del is able to play as much as he does. And when he makes a big run or another first down, I can cheer for him and mean it. I don't want that to be any different." He spoke earnestly. "I'm afraid all that old trouble and jealousy will come back if I let myself think and talk about the fact that I'm not getting to play very much these days." He expelled his breath with a rush. "You understand what I'm trying to say, don't you?"

She nodded. She was proud of him for caring more about being close to Del than getting to play every minute of every game. She thought that was one of the things that made her like Doug so much. He had convictions and wasn't about to be swayed from them. Seeing his strength of character made her want to walk closer to Jesus, although she wouldn't tell that to Doug. As they crossed the street, she looked up at him approvingly.

* * *

Del and Doug had almost given up ever getting to meet Virgil Trumbo. Twice they had called the Trumbo home for him and stopped by once on their way to the library, but they were never able to find him at home. They had about given up getting to meet him during the football season when Kay informed them that the Trumbo family would be over for dinner the following Sunday noon.

"That's great," Doug exclaimed.

Del glanced impishly at Danny. "So we are going to get to talk to him after all," he said. "The great professional football player really exists."

"Why, did you think he didn't?"

"We were beginning to wonder. We were beginning to think that you'd made him up."

"Del!" DeeDee protested. "You know Danny wouldn't do that."

"I *thought* I knew he wouldn't do a thing like that," her brother continued. "But you've got to admit it does look mighty strange. It's been weeks since the Trumbo family moved to town, and we haven't been able to meet Mr. Trumbo yet."

"If you can just wait until Sunday," Kay said, "you can meet him and ask him all the questions about football you want to know."

"Now, wait a minute, Kay," Danny said. "After all, Virge is just going to be here for the afternoon. We didn't invite them for a month."

She turned back to her sewing. "I hope he won't be bored with all that football talk."

"He won't be." Doug spoke confidently. "I've never met him, but I can tell you that much right now. He won't get bored talking about football."

As soon as the Trumbos arrived and the boys were introduced to the broad-shouldered missionary, they started throwing questions at him. They wanted to know what it was like playing pro ball, whether the game was as rough and demanding as it seemed to be on TV, and how much tougher the pro circuit really was than the southern conference he played in when he went to college.

Doug had been right about Virgil enjoying the football conversation. He answered their questions in as much detail as he could and entertained them with story after story of his experiences playing big-time football. The Davis boys were entranced. Before either of them realized it, the afternoon was practically gone. Only then, just before Virgil and his family were to leave for home, did they ask him the question that had been in mind since they first met him.

"We were talking with the coach a couple of weeks ago," Del began. "He'd like to have you come down to the school some time and attend one of our practices. He'd like to meet you, and I think he'd like to have you talk with the guys."

"I know. I had a call from him yesterday."

"Then you'll come and give us some pointers?" Doug asked.

"I might be able to," the former pro replied. "I'll have to see about that in a week or two." He put on his jacket. "But I am going to be speaking at your athletic banquet this year. That's what he called me about."

"That's great!" Del exclaimed.

"I really hate to take the time," he continued, "but it will give me a tremendous opportunity to witness."

They were all ready to leave when Kay was able to persuade them to stay for supper, assuring them it would only take a few minutes. Danny and Virgil went to the living room and sat down, while Del and Doug went down to the family room in the basement. Gary, who was sprawled on the couch reading, stopped and looked up.

"You know, Gary," Doug said, "your dad's a great guy!"

His eyes gleamed. "You're sure not going to get me into an argument about that!"

"It's great that you've moved here to Rock Point for this year."

"I think so, too. In fact our whole family thinks so. Dad and Mom say it's really an answer to prayer that Patti and I can go to school here all year."

Del and Doug fell silent. They both thought back to the way things were when their parents were alive. Of course, they were only in grade school then, being homeschooled when they weren't home on furlough, but they could remember the long conversations their parents had about schooling for them. They wondered what it would have been like if their parents had lived and they were faced with getting their education on the mission field.

CHAPTER 6

INVITATION TO A PARTY

Del was with Letitia as much as time would permit during the football season. The coach didn't like having the guys date and told them so, but he didn't call them in and talk to them about it as long as they didn't date during the week. Del and Letitia usually tried to find something to do together on Saturday night, and occasionally he took her to church Sunday evening.

They often went to a concert or something for the high school kids at one of the Rock Point churches. On other occasions they rode around and wound up at the Hitching Post or a drive-in where the kids hung out. More often they double dated with Doug and Tina.

Del felt more comfortable with Letitia than with any other girl he knew. They had never talked about dating exclusively, but it seemed that neither of them went out with anyone else.

He saw again and again the change that had come into Letitia's life. It wasn't that she talked continually about her faith in God or what Jesus Christ had done for her. Far from it. The change was more subtle than that and showed itself in many little ways. It seemed to affect every corner of her life.

Actually, it seemed to Del that Letitia was far more fun to be with than ever before. For one thing, she wasn't feeling sorry for herself, and he could talk to her without the risk of offending her. The way it used to be, she seemed to spend most of her time feeling bad about something he had said or hadn't said. Now she didn't take every casual remark seriously. And when they did get to talking about the things of God, which often happened, there was a radiance that shone through everything she said. He had never known anyone else who was quite as quick to take every opportunity to witness to those around her.

Del wasn't the only one who was aware of the change that had come into Letitia's life. A lot of the other kids didn't know why she was different. All they were aware of was that she had suddenly blossomed into a likable girl. Since September she had more friends than ever before. Kids who had only greeted her in the hall when she was a sophomore and a junior soon were in her circle of friends, and she was soon among the most popular girls in school.

Not everyone was drawn to her now that Jesus Christ had given her a new life. Some laughed at her commitment, and others were repulsed and scornful. Among them were several of the guys on the football squad. More than one talked with Del about her, professing not to be able to understand how he could go out with her.

"You don't mean to tell me that you still go out with that oddball Letitia Warren, do you, Del?" one of them asked.

Del finished tying his shoes and looked up. "Sure," he said. "We go out together whenever we have the chance. She's a lot of fun to be with."

"I can't see that. She's such a kook on religion, I'd think she would drive you buggy."

Del had never talked with any of the guys about Jesus Christ in the locker room before. Just thinking about it brought the sweat out on his forehead. But he had to defend Letitia. He couldn't have anybody talking about her, even though they weren't saying anything that would harm her character.

"I wouldn't say she's such an oddball," Del countered. "To tell you the truth, what she says about Jesus Christ makes a lot of sense."

By this time several nearby had stopped what they were doing and listened.

"I didn't know you were one of that kind, too!" the boy retorted.

"But I am!" Del was surprised at the fervor in his

voice. "I believe exactly the same way Letitia does. I've put my trust in Jesus Christ, too."

The other boy shook his head as though he had difficulty in believing what Del said. "I've been playin' football with you all year and I've never heard anything about it before right now. You're a regular guy, Del. You don't seem like a religious nut at all."

Del colored. "A guy doesn't have to be a nut to believe in Jesus Christ."

Del thought the guys would start needling him about his faith, but they didn't. In fact, they seemed to have more respect for him. But that wasn't true as far as he was concerned. To think, the guys had played football with him all year and didn't even know he was a Christian!

* * *

Hank Warren was more disturbed than anyone else by the change that had come over his sister in recent months. He didn't say much about her to his parents, but when the guys at school started asking about her, he was defensive and apologetic.

"She's sure a different girl than she used to be," one of the guys told him. "Or haven't you noticed?"

"I haven't noticed any big change in her," he lied. "What makes you think I would?"

"Come off it, Hank. You know what she's like now. She's a real weirdo."

His face flushed, and he stammered defensively as he tried to explain away the things they were saying about his sister. "She's about the same around home as she's always been. I haven't seen anything so much different about her." He would have gone on down the hall, but the guys called him back.

"If you haven't, you're the only one. Everybody in school's talking about her. She's a nut – a religious fanatic!"

His cheeks paled, and he shuffled nervously from one foot to the other. "Oh, that," he answered. "She was on a Jesus kick while she was in the hospital, but she's getting over it now." He managed a thin laugh. "I didn't know what you were talking about at first."

They knew he was upset and weren't going to let him off so easily. "That's not the way we've been hearing it. I figured she'd have your whole family converted by this time – and especially you. You act like just the kind who'd fall for that stuff."

"Guess again." He swore to let them know how far he was from accepting Letitia's Savior.

"You heard what happened in English class a couple of weeks ago, didn't you?"

Hank had heard. Everybody in school had heard about it. But he wasn't about to admit it and have them razz him about that, too.

"What English class?"

"Go ahead," someone else put in. "Tell him."

"She got up and read her theme about this new

religion of hers, and half the kids in the class were bawling before she got done." He snickered. "It turned out to be a regular evangelistic service."

"You can't pay any attention to that. She gets carried away when she starts writing. She's always been that way. You can't pay any attention to what she puts on paper."

At that someone else broke in. "The way I get it, she tries to convert everybody she can. They're calling her the school chaplain." He laughed mockingly. "I'd been planning on asking her for a date, but I sure wouldn't go out with her now. I wouldn't date her for five hundred bucks."

Hank bristled, and he wiped the moisture from his forehead with a trembling hand.

"Just lay off talking about my sister, okay? She may be a little kooky when it comes to religion, but I'm not goin' to have you guys talk about her!"

They stared at him.

"I knew she'd be getting to you. One of these days she'll have you on your knees praying too!"

"That I'd have to see!" one of Hank's friends laughed. "Call me up when it happens so I can come over and get some pictures, okay, Hank?"

He swore again. "I've heard all the talk I'm going to listen to about Letitia and her religion! What she believes is her business. It's nothing to you. Understand?"

For a while after that, the guys teased him, asking

him how many altar calls he had answered. But they were careful not to say too much about his sister. He was a big guy, and they didn't want to have trouble with him.

He tried to pretend that it didn't bother him when they teased him. He even joked about it occasionally. But it did get him uptight. There was no getting around that. Every time they razzed him, he was even more determined than ever not to let Letitia get her hooks into him. He wasn't buying that religion she was always talking about. She could quit trying.

When she first came home from the hospital, she had asked her dad if it would be all right for her to return thanks at mealtime before they ate. They had never done it before, and she didn't know what he would think about it. However, he agreed readily. At that moment he would have agreed to most anything she suggested, he was so glad to have her back home once more.

"If that's what you want to do, Letitia," he said, "It's fine with me. We've sure got a lot to be thankful for these days, the way you're getting along and all."

Her mother nodded. "I think it would be nice to say grace before we eat. After all, we are a religious family."

Both Letitia and Hank cringed at that, but they didn't say anything.

At first the whole family liked the fact that they prayed before eating, but after the guys at school started razzing Hank about his sister's religion, the simple little prayer irked him.

"Do you *have* to pray at every meal, Letitia?" he asked, wrinkling his nose distastefully.

His dad came to her defense. "Now, Hank, we've had enough of that. It doesn't hurt any of us to thank the good Lord once in a while for what He gives us."

The boy glanced up at him questioningly. He hadn't expected him to say what he did. It sure didn't sound like him.

"Are you going off on that stupid religion of hers, too, Dad? That I didn't expect."

His dad's cheeks colored. "It probably wouldn't hurt any of us to have a little more of what Letitia's got. She shows us all up when it comes to being happy and living the way a person ought to live."

Hank's mouth tightened. "I didn't think I was such a bad guy."

Letitia, who had been sitting there motionless and silent, listening to them, knew that her cheeks were flaming. She ached for Hank. She was so concerned that he would yield his life to Jesus Christ, and the more she prayed for him, the farther away from God he seemed to be. She saw that he was watching her, and she turned quickly away, hoping to keep him from seeing the hurt in her face.

"Let's change the subject, shall we?" Mrs. Warren suggested.

"Good idea," Hank muttered. Letitia was upset,

and he knew why. It bothered him to have her look as though she was about to cry and know that he was the cause of it. She was a great kid, just about as nice a sister as any guy could have. He'd have busted anyone else in the mouth for making her feel as bad as he had that evening.

If only she wasn't so ape over religion that she had to go around preaching to everybody, Hank thought. It wasn't her praying before they ate that got to him. A lot of people did that without letting it ruin them. It was nothing to get so uptight about. It was all that other junk that went with it.

And the way she prayed! That got to him. It was as though she was really talking to Someone she knew and loved. If he wasn't careful, he'd be buying the same religion she had, and the guys would be on his back. He had plenty of reason to be mad.

That was another thing about Letitia that he couldn't understand. It used to be she was mad or feeling bad about something most of the time. The whole family was afraid to say anything to her for fear of setting her off. When that happened, she was likely to bawl for hours.

She wasn't that way now. She didn't get mad or feel uptight about all the pain and trouble she'd had since the accident. If she did anything, she would be humming to herself or singing one of those religious songs the kooks at church liked so much. And she was always so cheerful and thoughtful anymore.

That was the kind of stuff that got to him. It wasn't any wonder he was upset when she insisted on praying at the table before they ate. Lately he couldn't be around her for thirty minutes without having something happen to make him feel as though he was a real creep. Even at night the things Letitia had said and did continued to bother him. He had trouble getting to sleep, and more than once he woke up disturbed.

It wasn't that he was such a terrible character. Most of the kids at Northwest High would say he lived a clean life. Some would call him odd. He didn't drink or smoke or fool around with drugs. And the girls he went with said he was always a gentleman when they were out with him.

In fact, until Letitia had come home from the hospital and was so different, he had always considered himself to be a pretty good guy. It was only in the face of the change that had come into her life that he realized the shallowness of his goodness. Just being around his sister made him realize what a phony he was and how much selfishness controlled his life. It made him mad just thinking about it.

In the days that followed he tried to act as though he really hadn't seen any change in his sister and that her faith didn't really mean anything. It would disappear as soon as she was able to put aside her crutches and live a normal life. It probably wouldn't be long until she would be crying half the time or curled up in a corner feeling sorry for herself.

He really didn't want her to be that way. He was excited and pleased when he saw that she had so many new friends now that she had come out of her shell. If she could only keep that part of the new Letitia and get rid of that religion bit, everything would be perfect. He was sure that one of those days she would let her Christian religion slip off and the guys wouldn't be able to give him such a bad time.

That was not the case, however. As the weeks went by, she was still as stable and as radiant as ever. Her smile was quick and continuous. And she was quick to tell anyone who would listen that Jesus Christ was the One who had made the change in her life.

Hank had to admit that he enjoyed being with her more now than he ever had before. He had always loved her. That was the reason he had been so disturbed by the way she used to pull herself into a shell and refuse to come out or make friends. And when she cried for hours on end, it had upset him so much he would have done most anything to get her straightened out. That was why he got DeeDee Davis to befriend her.

Hank had to admit he himself was responsible for Letitia being so religious. She had gotten it from DeeDee, he was sure. It had stopped her from crying all the time and had solved her problems. Her religion had made her fun to be with – and that was something he couldn't have said a few months before.

In spite of that, he had avoided being alone with

her as much as possible the last few weeks. He *had* to stay away from her if he was going to avoid being swallowed up by that new faith of hers.

Some of the kids at school were drawn to God by her talking to them. Others were turned off by it, like the guys who razzed Hank so much. He tried to change the subject when they taunted him, but that was useless. The more he tried to convince them that he was no more religious than they were, the more fiercely they prodded him.

"We were going to ask you to come to our party next Friday night," one of the guys said, "but you're so religious now that you wouldn't be interested."

His temper flamed. "How do you know I wouldn't be interested?"

"You're such a good boy now, that you wouldn't approve of *our* kind of a party."

Hank didn't know why he fell for their trick. Even as he talked to them about the party, he knew that he really didn't want to go to it. He never had liked parties that were so wild they had to be held in secret. But even though he didn't want to go, he found himself drawn into it, even helping them make their plans.

He was mad at himself for it, but he had to do something to get them to ease off.

"I still don't think you'll come," one of the guys said. "When it gets right down to it, you'll chicken out."

Hank flushed scarlet. "Try me!" he exploded.

"Just try me before you get so sure of what I'll do and what I won't."

"Okay. Okay. If that's what you want, we will. If you come to our beer bash, we'll know that we're all wrong about that religion of Letitia's. We'll know it's not getting to you after all."

"I'll be there."

"I'll believe it when I see you with a can of beer in your hand."

"I don't know what kind of a guy you take me for," Hank muttered.

"That's what we've been trying to tell you." His laughter rang along the corridor. "We take you for a religious fanatic like your sister."

"You'll find out!" In that moment he didn't care what kind of a party he had been invited to.

CHAPTER 7

HANK'S CONFLICT

Hank Warren hadn't decided to go to the beer party because he wanted to. He finally told them he would be there so they would ease off teasing him. In spite of his athletic skill and his size, Hank was never quite sure of himself. Like his sister before her conversion, Hank carried great quantities of self-doubt within. The approval of his friends and even his acquaintances was very important to him. When he felt himself slipping in their esteem, he grasped desperately at a chance to gain back their respect.

"We're finally gettin' Hank wised up," Glen Elwood sneered. "Now, if we can only get him out on a few double dates to complete his education, we'll make a *real* man out of him."

Anger blazed in Hank's eyes. "Can it, Glen!"

"Don't get so uptight, man. Your education is about to begin."

A slow red climbed into Hank's cheeks and spread across his forehead. His fists knotted until the veins corded the back of his hands.

Elwood's pimply face cracked into a grin. But he didn't say anymore. He was a head shorter than Hank and as skinny as a pencil. Razzing the guys was one thing. Standing up to them when he had them mad enough to sharpen his feet and pound him into the ground was something else. He had a certain cunning about him and a knack for sensing how far he could go. He had reached that point with Hank.

"Did I tell you about the date I had last week?" he asked his audience, changing the subject deliberately. "Wow!"

Hank spun on his heel and stormed away. He didn't know why it mattered to him what Glen thought about him. If only that sharp-tongued little terrier hadn't kept yipping about Letitia's religion and Hank being a fanatic, too. He could take most anything but that!

Out in the parking lot, Hank yanked open the door of his car and threw his books across the seat. Once in, he turned the key in the ignition, gunned the motor, and roared off.

As he drove considerably faster than the speed limit, he began to think about Letitia. Actually, she was as much at fault as Glen and the others. If she hadn't tried to save the world, that bunch of guys wouldn't even know she was a Christian. They didn't have any time for girls like her. Until she started preaching to everyone in sight, they didn't know she was alive. Having her after him all the time about her religion was bad enough. Now she had bugged his friends so much they were making him miserable. When Hank got home an hour or two later, Letitia was sitting in the living room, a book open on her lap.

"Hi, Hank," she sang out brightly.

He scowled and headed for his room.

"Is something wrong?" she called after him.

"Lay off, will you?" He slammed the door savagely.

Hank hadn't expected that Letitia would get word of the beer bash, at least for a while. He knew he wasn't going to say anything to her or anyone else about it, and he didn't think the other guys would either. It wasn't the kind of thing a guy wanted people to know about.

But the story leaked out. He supposed that mouthy Glen Elwood told somebody. Anyway, Letitia heard about it and the fact that he had agreed to go. She mentioned it to him the next evening when they were alone in the family room.

"For cryin' out loud!" he exploded. "Don't talk so loud! You'll have Mom and Dad both on my neck."

"Are you going to that beer party, Hank?"

"What makes you think I'd go to a party like that?" he hedged. "Have I ever?" He didn't lie to her outright, but he did everything he could to make her think he wasn't.

She read the truth in his eyes, and the hurt

deepened until she could scarcely allow herself to think about it. There was no need to question him.

"You are going, aren't you?"

"What if I am?" he snarled. "I don't have to answer to you for everything I do. You're not my jailor, Letitia, even though you seem to think you are!"

"I happen to care a lot about you and what you do, Hank," Letitia said, looking him straight in the eye.

"Yeah," he retorted bitterly. "You care so much about me you're in my hair all the time. If you had your way, I'd never do anything except sit around reading the Bible and praying the way you do."

"That isn't fair!"

"You bet it isn't! You just let me take care of myself. Okay?"

Hank slammed his book shut and stood up.

She would probably bawl for an hour or so, he told himself, but she had to learn that she couldn't run his life. He didn't try to tell her what to do. Why did she have to get on his back as though she owned him?

He was about to leave when a sobering thought ducked in at one corner of his mind. Now that she *knew* about the beer bash and that he was planning to go, she could give him a real bad time. He would never have had to concern himself with her betraying him before, no matter what he planned on doing. If anything, she'd have helped him deceive their parents. She was so religious now that he couldn't be sure about anything that had to do with her. She'd probably figure keeping quiet was the same as a lie.

"I suppose you're going to tell mom and dad."

"Please don't go, Hank," she said evasively.

He moved closer to her. "Are you going to tell them, or aren't you?"

"You know what'll happen to you if they find out. Dad is so set against drinking that he'll ground you for sure. He might even make you sell your car."

He stared accusingly at her. When she was in the hospital, he vowed he would never lose his temper with her again if only she got out and was able to walk again. She was only beginning to get along without her crutches and he was more furious at her than he had ever been in his life. But he had reason to be mad, he decided. A guy's own sister threatening to squeal on him! Who wouldn't get uptight?

"Don't get so upset," he lied. "I just told the guys I'd go to keep them from pesterin' me. The chances are I won't make it."

She didn't tell him she knew he wasn't telling the truth, but he wasn't deceiving her.

"I've been praying and praying for you."

He flushed self-consciously and edged away. When she started that preaching, it was time to split. "I've got to be going."

Letitia sensed his new irritation, but she couldn't help it. She had to go on. "I've been so anxious for you to let Jesus Christ have control of your life, Hank, and you seem to get farther away all the time." The words clung to the roof of her mouth, and she had to force them out. "Is there something in my life that has kept you away?"

"What do you mean by that?"

"If–If there's anything that I'm doing or not doing that's a hindrance to you," she stammered, "please forgive me."

He had wanted to leave when she first got on the subject of religion. Now he was desperate to get away. He couldn't see what she was so uptight about. The idea of her apologizing to him was ridiculous. She hadn't done anything to turn him away from that faith of hers.

"I've got to split," he replied. "I've got a quiz to study for."

With that he turned away from her, but she called him back. "I want you to know that I'll be praying that you don't go."

"I've already told you a dozen times that I don't think I will."

She brushed the remark aside. "And if you do go, I'm going to pray that you'll have a miserable time every minute that you're there! And that mom and dad will find out about it!"

He flushed scarlet. The kind of a connection she had with God, it sounded as though he didn't have a chance. If he went, he'd be sure to wind up in jail or in big trouble with his dad. "Are you going to tell on me or not? That's what I want to know."

Her gaze met his evenly, and he thought he saw fire in her eyes. "I haven't decided yet."

Letitia really didn't know whether she could go to their parents about the beer party or not. She had never told on Hank before, even as a little kid. There were times when she had been punished for things he had done, but she remained silent. When he got so mad and belligerent himself, she felt like going to Dad, but she didn't think she could. There had to be some other way.

The next morning she saw Bill Anderson in the hall, and he came over to help her up the stairs. She planned to share her concern for Hank with Del at noon, but almost before she realized what she was doing, she was telling her companion of her special concern for her brother.

"Did you *ever* get to talk to him about Jesus and what He's done in your life?" she asked.

Bill hesitated. He didn't like telling her the truth, but he had to. He had never even tried to share Christ with Hank. To be completely honest, he hadn't even prayed for him more than a few times.

"But I will," he answered firmly. "I'll talk to him before the party."

Her thanks flashed in a quick smile.

* * *

Hank was as disturbed by his talk with his sister as she was, but for a different reason. For the next couple of nights he tossed restlessly in bed. The more he thought about it, the more convinced he became that she would tell his mom and dad about the beer party.

Her thinking was so messed up, she would make herself believe it was her Christian duty to squeal on him and get him in trouble with their parents. That wouldn't be so good, either. He knew their dad as well as she did. And what she said about him was true enough. In fact, it was an understatement. If he learned about the beer bash, he would really lower the boom!

Hank was a high school senior, but that wouldn't make any difference to Dad. He'd ground him and take his wheels away from him for a starter. And there was no knowing what else he might do!

Finally, he became convinced that it would be stupid for him to go to a party like that anyway. He would be risking too much. Now that Letitia was onto it, he didn't have a chance of getting away with it.

He would never have told her, but in a way, he was glad she had gotten onto him about it. He had never really wanted to go out with the guys on a beer bash. She had just given him a good reason for not going. He'd tell them she would squeal on him if he went. They ought to be able to understand a reason like that.

The following morning on the way to school, he told her about his decision. She eyed him questioningly.

"I shouldn't doubt you, Hank, but are you telling me the truth?" she asked, finding it difficult to believe that she no longer had to be concerned about Hank going to the party.

"What can I say to make you believe me? I've finally made up my mind, that's all. I'm not going."

Her eyes shone. "Did Bill talk to you?"

He glanced suspiciously at her. "Bill who?"

"Bill Anderson."

His grip tightened on the wheel. "For cryin' out loud, Letitia!" he exploded. "You didn't ask Bill to pour the heat on me, did you?"

Her smile left. "I–I had to have *someone* to talk to."

"Who else did you draft into your little game?"

She hesitated.

"Del Davis?"

She didn't want to tell him, but she could not keep from it. She couldn't lie to him. "I did mention it to Del," she said lamely.

He was furious. "I suppose you got that whole bunch of girls you run around with to pray about it?"

She did not answer him.

"If you weren't my sister, I'd–" He pounded the steering wheel with his fist. "Don't you see what you're doing to me? You've made me the fool of Northwest High. I'll probably get laughed right off the football team!"

"They won't say anything."

"Hah!"

"I'm sorry, Hank. I didn't want to make anybody laugh at you. I just wanted to keep you from hurting yourself."

"You've taken care of that by doing it for me."

Now that he learned what Letitia had done, he was more convinced than ever that he had to get out of that beer bash. Half the kids at school knew he had been invited. If he went, they'd all know about it, and it wouldn't be long until his dad found out. That is, if Letitia didn't tell him! He supposed that would be just about like her.

He wanted to find the guys as quickly as possible and see whether they bought what he told them or not. That really didn't make any difference now. Letitia had fixed him – good.

He looked for them at their usual hangouts in the building, but they weren't there that morning. One of the guys told him, with a wink, that Glen and Little Joe had some pickups to make that morning so they could be cold for the party that night.

"You're goin' to be there tonight, aren't you?"

"That's what I wanted to talk to Joe about."

"You'd better change your mind and stay away."

Hank's bony features paled. Had the story of what Letitia had done beaten him to school? "What makes you say that?"

"I just bet Glen a six pack that you wouldn't show tonight."

"You don't care much about your money, do you?" He didn't mean to say that. The words popped out.

"I figured you'd come at us with some wild yarn about that sister of yours threatening to tell your parents on you if you go."

"You don't know me very well, do you?"

"I wouldn't say that. The way I figure it, you'll try to hide behind Letitia so you can get out of the beer bash without lettin' us know how religious you are."

Hank winced. Somebody talked. And no wonder. With all the kids that stupid sister of his told, she'd about as well have put the announcement on the bulletin board or on the PA system.

"I'm not hidin' behind anyone!" He spat out the words with an oath.

"Well, you'll have to prove it to me! When I see you drive up tonight, I'll believe you're coming and not before!"

CHAPTER 8

A LAST-MINUTE DECISION

Doug had been striving desperately to make the defensive starting lineup ever since he had been put on the defensive squad late in September. He could play the position well, but as the season wore on, everything worked against him.

Being good wasn't enough to nail down a starting position at Northwest, he discovered. A guy had to be better than good, especially when there were two others trying to get the same position. They were both rugged and bigger than he was, and they both had a lot of competitive spirit.

He did all right against them the first couple of weeks, however, and he began to think he might be able to nose them out. Then he pulled a leg muscle during the scrimmage and was kept out for one game. When he was able to play again, he discovered that missing practice had cost him some ground.

The other two tackles had turned in sharp performances the game he missed and were more firmly entrenched than ever. The Rock Point news station, which seldom had space for individual high school performances, was lavish in its praise of the defensive line and particularly the play at tackle. Doug had already prepared himself for the fact that he probably wouldn't get to play at all that Friday night.

He and Del were going home from the Thursday afternoon session when he shared his fears with his brother.

"And I really need the time if I'm going to earn a letter this year. The season's about over."

"You'll get in," Del told him confidently. "And you'll letter, too." He wished he was as positive of the truth in what he said as he tried to sound. He liked the football coach at Northwest, but for some reason the guy wasn't particularly high on Doug's ability. He acted as though he didn't think Doug quite had it.

That was something of a surprise to him. His brother had a lot of drive and a fierce desire to win. Del knew that he had a lot more drive than he had.

Both the Davis boys knew about the beer bash that was being held after the Friday night game and were concerned that Hank might go. It seemed that everyone in school knew about it. They couldn't spend much time thinking about it, however. They were both taken up with their classes and the game. They scarcely had time to pray about it as Letitia and DeeDee had urged them to.

* * *

Central won the toss and elected to receive. Doug glanced expectantly at the coach, but his name wasn't called to start at tackle. He went over to the bench and sat down. That was where he stayed for the entire first half.

It proved to be a hard-fought game, and Central spent most of the second quarter deep in Northwest's territory. Just before the gun sounded for half time, the regular starting tackle had the misfortune to crack a bone in his wrist. Midway in the third period there was trouble on the field, and his replacement threw a punch at the offensive guard. That was the end of Burton. The referee ejected him from the game. He came off the field dejectedly, unwilling to raise his head and look at the coach. That was one thing they had all been cautioned repeatedly about.

"If the other team can make you lose your cool," he had said to them often, "they've got half the victory."

The coach sent Burton to the showers immediately and had Doug take his place.

The fight and the way it ended seemed to fire up the Central High offense. They charged out of the huddle and blasted across the line of scrimmage to open a hole big enough for a two-ton truck. Doug saw what was happening and rolled aside to avoid the blocker who was charging at him. The ball carrier was a step behind him, and Doug was off balance.

But he righted himself and leaped desperately at the Central fullback, hauling him down on the twenty.

No one else was close enough to have done anything about it. If Doug had missed, Central would have gone all the way. As it was, they were stopped two yards short of a first down.

The next play was intended to be a pass. Doug read it correctly and dove through the line to smash the quarterback to the ground before he could get the ball away.

Now it was Northwest's turn to come alive. They held on the next two plays, forcing Central to try a field goal. The kicker was rushed, and the ball went wide. When Doug trotted off the field, the coach nodded in appreciation.

He sat down, grinning. This was more like it. It was the way he used to play back in Fairview, Minnesota. He didn't know why, but something had happened to him on that series of plays. He had suddenly found himself. He didn't know how long it would last, but he had a confidence out there that hadn't been his since they left their former school.

It was a good feeling.

As so often happens with football teams, the brilliant stand of the defensive unit sparked the offense. They started a drive on their own thirty-eight that ended eleven plays later with their first touchdown of the night. Del played an important part in the long drive. Before the fourth quarter was two minutes old, he had led them down to the door again and punched across, giving Northwest a narrow thirteen to ten lead.

Late in the final period, Doug saved the game once more. A short pass to the tight end was good, and the guy was as fast as a cheetah. He dodged past his first would-be tackler and sprinted for the goal. Doug didn't know where the speed came from or how he was able to shake himself free to pursue the ball carrier and tackle him within the ten-yard line. Thinking back, he decided the guy hadn't known he was coming and slacked off, but the reason didn't matter. He saved the game with that tackle.

A great roar went up from the stands as the teams lined up. Before Central was able to get another play away, the gun sounded. The game was over, and Northwest had won!

* * *

Tina Nicholson was waiting on the steps of the school building for Doug when he came out of the locker room after the game. She ran over to him and took his arm impulsively.

"Oh, Doug! I'm so proud of you! I *knew* you could do it!"

He grinned. For the first time since he had gone out for football at the large Rock Point high school, he was satisfied with the way he had played and was confident that he could do it again.

"Now the coach will have to let you start," she said exultantly. "He'll have to put you on the first string."

He did not argue with her about that. In fact, he had been thinking much the same thing. "I did have a pretty good night," he agreed. "Even if I do say so myself."

"A good night?" she exclaimed. "You were terrific! You should have heard the people in the stands. Everyone said that you won the game for us."

His smile left. "One person never wins a game, Tina. There were a lot of other guys out there giving everything they had. If I'd tried to do it myself, we'd have been whipped before the first quarter was over. Everybody had a hand in what happened tonight."

"I know, but *you* were the one who stopped Central's touchdown drives. If it hadn't been for you, they'd have scored twice, and we'd have been beaten."

He didn't like having her give him so much credit for what he had done. "Really, Tina," he said. "I was just lucky in being able to read the plays. That was the big thing that helped me to get in on those tackles. Anyone else could have done it if they'd been lucky."

"But they didn't! That's the point."

* * *

Letitia watched Hank silently as he put on his coat that evening before the game. He kept his back to her, thinking she was going to ask him where he was going after the football game. If she had planned on questioning him, he didn't give her a chance.

But it wouldn't have done her any good if she had tried to find out what he was going to do. He wouldn't have told her anything, and he wouldn't have let her persuade him to stay at home. He even had to run the risk of having her tell their parents on him. Regardless of what happened, he couldn't have the guys pouring the heat on him all the time. He didn't plan on going to any more beer bashes. He wouldn't have to. Once would be enough to prove to them that he wasn't a religious crackpot and get them off his back. That was all he wanted to do. And nobody could blame him for that.

He played a good game that night, too, although he didn't make a hero of himself the way Doug Davis had. He held up his end of things and got to play more than two quarters. He had earned his letter a couple of games ago, so getting to play now was just a bonus.

As soon as he dressed following the football game, he got into his car and headed up the mountains in the direction of the cabin where the beer bash was to be held. He could have ridden with one of the other guys, but he hadn't wanted to. Being at the party would be bad enough without listening to some pipsqueak like Glen yak about how much he was going to drink before it even started.

The cabin was a drive of thirty minutes away from town, but he was so upset that it seemed to take three times that long. At last he pulled into the yard. Three guys were already parked outside, and the place was ablaze with lights.

"Hey, guys! Look who's here!"

Several came out onto the porch to see.

"So you did come after all!" Glen shouted. "Come on in and have a beer!" He turned to the boy standing beside him. "You owe me a six-pack!"

"Okay. Okay. It was worth it. This is one bet I'm glad to pay off!"

"I didn't really think he'd come," Glen put in. "I figured he had too much religion to come out here and have some fun."

Hank got out of the car and started for the cabin reluctantly. With each step the heaviness in his heart increased. He didn't know when he had felt so miserable – or why. He was no longer concerning himself with the fact that his parents might find out he was there. It was more than that.

Almost to the porch, he stopped. *What am I doing here?* he asked himself silently.

In that moment he knew that he could not go in, regardless of what they said. The guys might razz him. They probably would pour it on more than ever, but that didn't make too much difference. He had to get out of there as fast as he could. He spun on his heel and started back toward his car.

His friends stared at him.

"Hey, Hank!" one of them called out. "What's the matter? Did you forget your Bible?"

"Lay off of him! He probably went back to get a case of beer out of his car."

But he opened the car door and got in. When he did that, they realized he was going to leave.

"I told you! I told you he was scared to come. He's got religion!"

Their laughter drifted to him over the night air as he started the engine and switched on the lights. He reached for the gear shift lever but stopped briefly. It still wasn't too late. He could go back to the party, even for a little while, and they would all soon forget that he had almost left.

If he did leave, he would be through as far as all the kids who counted for anything at Northwest were concerned. Everybody in school would get the message that he was a religious nut like his sister.

But that didn't stop him. He backed up a dozen feet, slammed his car into drive and roared away from the cabin, knowing as he did so, that the cost for his actions was high.

Now I've done it! he told himself as he headed down the long, twisting mountain lane toward the main road. He would be in for a razzing Monday when he went to school. Even the guys who hadn't been to the party would be on him about it.

At the moment he didn't care. They could think anything they wanted to about him. If they believed he was religious, they'd just have to think it until they found out different. He wasn't going to a wild party just to prove to his friends that he was an okay guy.

After the first burst of speed, he slowed and drove thoughtfully down the mountain and into Rock Point that lay at its foot. Without realizing quite where he was heading, he turned in the direction of Danny and Kay's. He wondered if DeeDee was home. She was as religious as Letitia, but for some reason they had always gotten on well together. She was one person he could talk to.

He didn't have any particular reason for wanting to talk to her. He sure wasn't interested in any more preaching. He'd had enough of that from his sister in the past few days to hold him for a couple of years. He guessed he was just upset and wanted to do something to take his mind off what had happened.

As he approached the block where Danny lived, he flicked on his turn signal and at the next intersection he headed toward town. He'd really make a fool of himself if he went up to the house to talk to DeeDee at this hour.

Then he remembered that there was a party at the church after the football game. Letitia had tried to talk him into going there instead of the beer bash. He laughed. It would really throw them all if he showed up at the church. They'd think they had a live one and would really panic.

That's what he ought to do, he mused. He should

march down to the basement where they were play-ing their Mickey Mouse games. Letitia would really be uptight! He'd give her the thrill of her life.

He drove down to the church and found a parking place. He had decided that he would go to the party there just for kicks. Del and Doug would be there and good old Bill Anderson. He was as flaked out on religion as Letitia was. And he could see DeeDee for a couple of minutes. He might not be able to talk to her long alone, but he didn't care too much about that.

Before he switched off the ignition, however, he decided against it. They would all get the wrong idea about his going to the church party, and they'd be on him harder than ever. Even Letitia would put on more heat than she had been, and it was bad enough around the house now. He'd be out of his skull to give her more encouragement to preach at him than she had already. He backed out onto the street once more. Being home would be better than going to a stupid Sunday school party.

He didn't go home right then, but drove around for a couple of hours until the lights were out at the church and his sister was home in bed. Leaving the beer bash hadn't eased the turmoil that churned within him. If anything, it was worse. And he didn't know why!

CHAPTER 9

HANK HAS QUESTIONS

The following Monday afternoon, Doug was surprised when he learned that the Rock Point news station had given him the coveted player-of-the-week award because of his superior play in the game against Central. The sports editor gave him credit for the victory just as Tina had done.

"It isn't often that a defensive tackle can be given credit for his team's winning a close game," the sportswriter said, "but last Friday night Doug Davis was the difference between two well-matched teams. He stepped into the gap and stopped two Central drives that would have given them the victory. And, as if that weren't enough, he stormed through a tough Central forward wall to nail the ball carriers on two successive plays, forcing them to try for a field goal. He was one of those who rushed the kicker, forcing the boot to go wide."

Doug said nothing about it to the rest of the family,

but Del looked up the article and read the account aloud at the dinner table that evening.

"That's really something!" he exclaimed.

"We were proud of the way both of you played Friday night," Danny added.

Del handed the article to his brother. "You ought to save that one."

Doug Davis shrugged. "It's not that big a deal."

"They never raved over me that way."

Doug was embarrassed. "They sure must've been short of news tonight to write like that. They've got to have something to fill the space."

"Oh, I wouldn't say that," Del countered. "Everybody at school was talking about the way you played Friday night. It was the most important game of the season, and you won it for us. I was really proud that you're my brother. I can tell you that right now."

Secretly, Doug was pleased, but it bothered him to hear Del talk that way.

"Lay off, will you?"

"I don't know why I should. It's the truth. You won the game for us."

"Yeah," he muttered. "Me and about thirty other guys."

* * *

The Monday night after the wild party, Hank came home early and went directly to his room. Right then, he didn't want to talk to anybody. He had such a rough day at school that he had wondered if it would ever end. Word of what had happened Friday night after the football game raced around school and wherever he went, guys were razzing him.

"You are in school this morning after all," Glen said to him.

"Why wouldn't I be?"

"I figured you'd still be sobering up."

"You know better than that," he retorted defensively.

Glen's laughter was cynical. "That's not the reason. I guess I was talking about myself. I figured you might have to go over to the church and scrub the floor or fold bulletins to pay for the terrible sin you committed Friday night by *almost* going to our party."

Listening to that sort of guff would have been bad enough from anyone. Hearing it from Glen was all but intolerable.

"Lay off!" he warned.

But Glen knew he had nothing to worry about. They were in the school building with hundreds of kids around. If Hank touched him, he could let out a yell and the big guy would be in worse trouble than he was in now.

"I can't say that I blame you," he continued. "I don't think I'd have gone to the party, either, if I'd been in your place. You'd have been a month working that off!"

His strident cackle attracted another guy who was there.

"I didn't think you'd dare to come to school today," the other boy said, "after what you did Friday night. I didn't think you'd face any of us."

Hank's temper flared. "It ought to be a guy's own business whether he goes to a party. I don't have to go around school taking a poll to see what I ought to do."

"Yeah, but don't ever try to tell us again that you haven't got 'religion.' You're as flaked out as your sister ever was."

That was only the beginning. Wherever he went, they were after him. In the hall it was a word or two, muttered as they met or passed him. In the classroom it was a sneer or a snickering little laugh. He cringed under the attack but said nothing. He had already learned that arguing with them only made things worse.

When he got home that afternoon, Letitia was there alone. He realized his mistake in going in as soon as he entered and saw that his mother wasn't there.

Now he was in for it.

She followed him to his room, ignoring his frown of disapproval.

"You don't know how happy I was when I got to school this morning and found out that you hadn't gone to the party. I had prayed and prayed that you wouldn't go, but I was so afraid you would that I–I have to confess I doubted God. I didn't believe He was going to answer my prayer, especially when you left the house Friday night before the game. I was so sure you were going out with the guys that I could have cried." She drew in a deep breath. "But you didn't! I was so happy, I did cry when I heard what happened. I didn't want to, but I couldn't help it."

"I didn't go to the party." He gestured irritably. "So, that's that. Just forget it. There's no need to make such a big deal of it!"

Letitia seemed ready to talk some more, but he wasn't about to have that. He'd had all the guff he wanted for one day.

Quickly, Hank went over to his desk and picked up his history book. He hadn't figured on studying until after dinner. There wasn't anything too pressing for his classes the next day, but he got out his books and opened them. Studying was a lot better than listening to that sister of his talk on and on.

* * *

When the Christian kids at school heard that Hank Warren had driven out to Glen's party but hadn't gone in, they began to wonder if he had made a decision for Christ. At their youth meeting, Bill Anderson and a couple of others asked Letitia about him.

"I wish he had." Her voice trembled. "But he says he doesn't need God. He can live a good life without Him. He seems to feel that he can do everything on his own."

Danny, who was leading the group, spoke up. "We know how concerned Letitia is for her brother. We've all been praying for him, but have we been doing anything more than that? Have we been concerned enough for Hank that we've made an effort to lead him to Christ?"

"What do you mean?" DeeDee asked.

"Has anyone besides his sister shared Jesus Christ with him?"

Letitia glanced quickly at Bill Anderson and smiled. He looked quickly away. She had asked him a couple of times to tell Hank what Jesus had done for him, and he said he would. But he hadn't. He hadn't even prayed regularly for her brother.

A crimson flush came to his cheeks. When it came right down to it, he had never witnessed to anybody the way Letitia did. Except for the fact that he ran with Christian kids and went to church, he had never done anything to let anyone know he loved Jesus Christ.

* * *

For the next week Hank Warren made a determined effort to avoid being alone with Letitia. She had already caused him plenty of trouble. The guys at school were still taunting him. He ducked them whenever he could, but a lot of times that wasn't possible.

That sister of his was going to have to learn that

he wasn't buying the religion that meant so much to her. He hadn't gone to Glen's party, but that didn't give her any reason to get so excited about it. It didn't mean that he was about to line himself up with all the freaks in school. He didn't care what she said to him, he wasn't about to get down on his knees and make a fool of himself the way she had.

It wasn't that Letitia had said so much more to him about making a decision for Christ. She had always used every chance she got to put in a word or two. Still, he had problems getting to sleep at night. Whenever he closed his eyes, he could see that look on her face when she told him that she knew he hadn't gone to the party with the guys.

He couldn't figure out why she had been so happy because of the things he did or didn't do. He didn't give her a bad time about running around with those church kids, although he thought most of them were pretty stupid. He didn't know why being around her filled his heart with such uneasiness either.

Hank was able to understand why Letitia got so hooked on religion. She felt as though she had been the source of all her parents' problems, and she had been so shy and introverted at school, she hadn't made friends. And, as if that wasn't enough, she had gotten all busted up on the ski trip last spring. It was simple to see why she turned to God. She needed a lot of help.

That didn't mean it was for him. He was getting

along fine the way he was. He was living a life that was good enough to get by. He didn't need a savior, and he didn't need a crutch. He had already decided that. As soon as she realized exactly how things were with him, the better they would get along.

Although he was positive he didn't need salvation or want it, he could not escape the emptiness in his heart. He didn't like having to admit it, but he was disturbed by the vague longing deep inside. He had been fighting it for months, but there was no doubting the fact that she had something he didn't have.

He had heard plenty of kids at school who made fun of her for the oddball things she believed and talked about with anyone who would listen, but she didn't fit the pattern they had cut out for her. For one thing, she wasn't obnoxious in her witnessing to anyone except him. She was careful who she talked to and how she told them about Jesus Christ and what He had done for her.

And she was happy in spite of all that had happened to her. That was the big change he had seen. It was the thing that kept gnawing at him.

He didn't know when he first decided that he would like to talk to somebody – to find out a lot of things about becoming a Christian that he didn't understand. One morning when he got up, he knew he had to get some answers from somebody.

He went to her door and knocked on it, but by the time she answered, he had lost his nerve.

"Did you want something, Hank?" she asked.

And there was that smile again!

"Yeah," he said. "Yeah, have you seen anything of my history book?"

"It's in the family room, Hank," she said, giving him a puzzled look.

If she ever knew he had another reason for knocking at her door, she said nothing about it.

As the days passed, the pressure within him continued to build. He had to talk to someone! He decided that. But who?

He could go to the pastor, he supposed, or to Danny Orlis or the youth minister at the church. Any one of them would be glad to talk to him. They could answer his questions too.

Still, he wasn't all that sure he wanted to get involved with them. He wanted a little information, but he didn't want that much. And he sure didn't want to get himself any more pressure. He had already had his fill of that.

If it wasn't for the pressure, he could talk to Letitia. She acted as though she knew all there was to know about the Bible. But talking to her about such things would be like pouring gas on a fire.

What he really wanted, he decided, was to talk to a guy about his own age – someone like Doug or Del Davis. He played football with them and knew them both well, so either would be all right, but it would be a little better to get Del to tell him what he wanted to know. He knew Del best. And why shouldn't he? The guy was coming over to see his sister all the time.

He had never heard Del say much about being a Christian, but so much the better. Hank preferred somebody who wasn't so pushy. He figured Del was a Christian because he was in church and Sunday school all the time and never missed a youth meeting. Besides, Letitia dated him. Hank knew his sister well enough to know she wouldn't be going out with anybody who didn't believe the way she did.

CHAPTER 10

BILL TALKS TO THE TEAM

Once Hank made up his mind to get information from Del, he sought him out in the hall.

"What are you going to be doing tonight when school's out? There isn't any football practice today."

"I know. Letitia and I were going to celebrate the afternoon off by going to the Hitching Post, but she just informed me she can't make it. She's going to the library to do some reading for a paper."

Hank grinned. That was great. He'd been wondering how long it would take for them to get together.

"I'll meet you there and buy you a coke."

Del was surprised that Hank would want to be with him. It was the first time that had ever happened. There were times when he had the idea that Letitia's brother wanted to keep away from him. But he didn't ask about it.

When classes were out for the day, the two boys met

and went over to the little eating place not far from the school. Del would have ducked into a booth near the front, but his companion led him to a secluded spot near the back. They ordered something cold to drink, and he waited for Hank to begin.

"How are things going, Del?" Hank asked, his voice tremoring slightly. He didn't know why he had asked such a stupid question, but the words popped out.

Del eyed him questioningly. "Fine. How about you?"

"Yeah, great."

The silence hung like a curtain between them.

Hank hadn't expected this. He thought it would be easy to talk with Del. He'd never had any trouble discussing things with him before.

"It sure is good to see how Letitia's doing, isn't it?"

The Davis boy's gaze narrowed. He wasn't quite sure how Hank meant that – whether he was talking about the way her back was improving or the spiritual change that had come over her. To him, both seemed phenomenal. "She sure gets around great. For a long time, I wondered if she would ever be able to walk again. Now she hardly ever has to use her crutches."

"That's right. I think she's surprised everybody by the way she's improving. She's not the same person at home anymore."

There was a strange wistfulness in his manner, a hesitance that indicated he wasn't talking about his sister's back at all. But it couldn't be that Hank wanted to talk about her spiritual condition, Del decided.

Her brother had never shown any interest in things like that. Del figured that he had to be careful. He didn't want to turn Hank off, now that he showed some signs of wanting to be friends with him.

He struggled inwardly, trying to decide what to say. Hank Warren wouldn't be the easiest guy to try to talk to about his need of Jesus Christ. Del knew how he had treated Letitia when she witnessed to him. It wouldn't do Hank any good if that happened.

The last time he and Letitia had been together, she asked him to pray for her brother, that he would see his own lost condition and the fact that he had to give his life to Jesus Christ if he was going to be truly happy. Del promised her he would pray for her brother.

In a way, it was thrilling to have the guy actually approach him. Still, it was disturbing. He didn't know quite what to say or how far to go. It wasn't going to help Hank if he made him mad trying to talk about his own spiritual need.

While Del was considering the matter, another guy they both knew joined them.

"Okay if I sit down?"

"Sure." Del scooted over, grateful for the reprieve.

Hank, on the other hand, didn't seem to feel the same way about it. Del had the firm impression that his companion didn't want to be disturbed by anyone else right then.

* * *

The last game of the football season was always one of the big ones for Rock Point Northwest. They had few traditional rivals, but Valley was one of them. For years the two teams had met to close the season and, as often as not, it was the deciding game for the conference championship.

However, it was one of those rivalries that didn't have to attract a great deal of attention. Everyone was interested in the Valley game, whether they followed Northwest sports or not, and the stands were always filled.

That year was no different than the others. Everyone was there, jamming into the stands until there was no room for anyone else. When the stands were filled, they stood at either end, crowding in one against another, until there was no more room even for standees.

Doug had played on the second and third string all season and had gotten to play only when one of the other two guys was injured or Northwest was so far ahead the entire second or third string was in. Yet, his showing the week before had been strong enough to earn him the starting position.

He continued the same startling play as that he exhibited in the last game. In the first five minutes of play he made two tackles and assisted on another that rocked Valley hard, forcing them to kick on fourth and nine, giving them the ball in good position.

The game was still an infant when Del got in. On his first carry he took a handoff from the quarterback and started around left end. A step from being tackled, he faked a lateral to the fullback who was charging up fast, avoided the outstretched arms of the Valley defensive end, and turned the corner for an important eleven yards.

Valley's defensive line moved into position and the Northwest quarterback fired a bullet pass into the flat where it was snaked in by the long arms of the wide end. The opposition, set for Del to carry the ball again, were caught flat-footed. Before they realized what was happening, Northwest scored and kicked the extra point.

After that, the rest of the first half was a grim, hard-fought battle. Valley came charging back, determined to score on that series of downs. They moved the ball to the Northwest twelve-yard line before the defense stiffened and they lost possession. Midway in the second period they reached the twenty before Doug pulled in a pass for his first interception of the year to stop the threat.

His play was not as spectacular as it had been the week before, but his play was solid. He was substituted quite often, but when he was in, he played a smart, determined game.

The Valley contest was almost a repetition of the

game the week before, except that when the game was over, the score was tied. Valley succeeded in running back a punt from their own twenty-nine-yard line to make the game seven to seven.

The Northwest coach called the guys together in the locker room. "One of the seniors wants to say something before we leave the locker room, but I'd like to talk to you now. This isn't the best season we've ever had by quite a ways. We've won five, lost two games, and tied this one. At a lot of schools a season like this would be considered excellent, but Northwest is used to winning."

He paused, looking from one to the other.

"But I want to tell you that this year's squad has been one of the best I've ever coached. I'm sure the entire staff agrees with me. You have proved yourselves to be real gentlemen, and I'm proud of you." He thanked them again and asked them all to wait for a few minutes when they were dressed.

Doug, who was tying his street shoes, looked up at his brother. "It's been a great season, hasn't it?"

"You can say that again. I enjoyed it a lot more than I did the last time. I can tell you that much."

A grin rested impishly on Doug's mouth. "That wouldn't happen to be because we got kicked off the squad and didn't get to play, would it?"

"That could have something to do with it," Del said, laughing. "But I was thinking about the season back in Fairview. I enjoyed playing there, too, but this year's been a lot more fun for me."

"There's one thing sure. You and I got along with each other a lot better than we did when we were playing in Fairview."

Del nodded. He guessed that was the real reason he enjoyed the football season so much more this year than the first year he played. He and Doug had been so jealous of each other then that it hadn't been much fun for either of them. Now, they not only weren't jealous of each other, they really enjoyed being together. It was more the way it had been when they were kids, only this was even better. He thanked God for it.

When everyone had showered and was dressed, the coach called them together. "Bill Anderson came to me the first of the week and asked if he could say a few words to you guys. Bill's a senior and has been playing with the first string for the past three years. I'm sure that what he's going to say will prove worthwhile."

There was a flurry of talking, but when Bill stood, the guys quieted so he could be heard. He squirmed uncomfortably under their curious stares.

"I–I've never been up before anybody to talk before," he began lamely, "and I'm scared half to death."

A couple of guys laughed sympathetically.

"But I've got to tell you something." He paused and began again. "First, I guess I'd better tell you what has happened to me lately. Some of you have probably noticed that I don't drink or smoke or swear anymore, but not many of you know why I'm different." He went on to tell them why the change came into his life.

"I've been praying for some of you ever since I gave my life to Jesus Christ, that you would do the same thing, but I've never had the nerve to talk to any of you personally. I want to ask your forgiveness for that."

Somebody snickered, but Bill was so intent he didn't even hear him.

He continued hesitantly, sharing his own experience as a new believer with them. He told them of the change Christ had brought into his life and what He could do for them if they would allow Him.

At first there had been skepticism and scorn in the eyes of the football squad, but as he went on, their cynicism turned to respect. Even the coach, whose profanity was unrestrained, was touched by what Bill said. When he finished, the coach thanked him quietly.

Del was stunned. He could scarcely believe that his ears were faithful in relating Bill's words to him. He and Doug had both been playing football for years and they had never once done anything like that. He hadn't even thought about it. And he wouldn't have had the nerve if he had.

Now Bill comes along and does it, and the guys take it from him. It made Del ashamed of himself.

He talked with Bill about it a few minutes later when they had a chance to be alone together just outside the school.

"It was great of you to do what you did tonight, Bill," he said. "You've got a lot of nerve."

The other boy pushed his compliment aside. "Don't say that! I haven't got any nerve at all. I was so scared when I was talking a few minutes ago, I was afraid I wouldn't be able to continue."

"But you did. That's the main thing."

"Letitia Warren is the one who presented Christ to me and made me see that I needed a Savior," Bill said, "but I couldn't even talk to Hank about Jesus, even after she asked me to." He told Del how he had confessed his failure to Letitia and asked her forgiveness. "Talking to the whole squad was the only way I could think of to get to him."

Del knew that Letitia had done a lot of talking to the kids at school, sharing Jesus Christ with them. He had known, too, that Bill Anderson was a new convert to Christianity, but he hadn't been aware of the fact that Letitia had been the one to present Christ to him. In a very real way she had been responsible for Bill's testimony to the football squad. It happened because she dared to present Jesus Christ to him and because she was so concerned about Hank that she asked Bill to talk to her brother.

And what about himself? Del had been a believer for years, but he had never done anything quite like Bill did. He wasn't even sure that all the guys on the squad even knew he was a believer.

In that moment he decided that he was going to Hank Warren the next day. He wasn't going to wait for the right opportunity. He was going to get him in the car and talk with him about Christ.

Waiting for the perfect chance was probably wise in most cases, he told himself, but the truth with him was that he wasn't actually waiting for the right time to speak. He was trying to find an excuse for keeping silent.

CHAPTER 11

"IT'S AS EASY AS ASKING"

Even before the incident in the locker room at school, Hank Warren knew about the change that had come over Bill Anderson. He had been one of the first to hear about it. He had been in the living room when Letitia called some of her Christian friends to pray for the new convert, but she hadn't said anything about leading Bill to Jesus Christ herself. That was one of the unusual things about his sister in the past few months. She didn't try to get credit for everything she did.

Hank was as surprised as Bill was to hear the response to the hesitant little locker room talk. The coach had thanked Bill for speaking to the football team, and the basketball squad, moved by what he said, decided to have prayer on the floor before their games. The sports reporter even mentioned it in his column.

It was then that Hank decided to talk to Bill. He didn't know why he hadn't thought of him before.

Bill Anderson was home when he called and asked him to go down to the Hitching Post with him that evening.

"I'd like to, Hank," he said, "but I don't know whether I ought to take the time tonight. I've got to study for a test tomorrow."

Hank could not conceal his disappointment. "Can't you take a few minutes? I really *have* to talk to you!"

Bill caught the urgency in the other boy's voice. "Sure thing. Stop by for me whenever you're ready."

"I'll be there in half a minute." Hank got his coat and started out to his car.

His mother wanted to know where he was going. "You've been out every night this week."

He was irritated by her protest. "I'll be back in a little while. I've got to see a guy."

Bill was waiting for him when he drove up. Hank wavered as the other boy came out of the house. It was clearly too late now. He would have to go through with this.

"Hi, Hank." Bill opened the door and slid in.

Hank turned the car in the direction of the highway.

"This isn't the way to the Hitching Post."

The Warren boy cleared his throat. "I really didn't want to go anywhere to eat. I've got to talk to you."

"What about?"

"I heard you in the locker room the other night."

Bill was almost apologetic. "I'm not so good at public speeches."

"It took a lot of nerve to stand up before that bunch and say what you did."

"That isn't what you called to talk to me about, is it?"

Hank cleared his throat. "Not exactly."

Bill squinted at him. For the first time he noticed that Hank was tense.

"What did you want to talk to me about?"

Silence was a wall between them. Hank had already decided how he was going to start, but now that they were together, everything fled, leaving his mind blank and empty.

"You did have something special you wanted to talk to me about, didn't you?"

He nodded. It had to come out now. He had gone too far to back down. Not that he wanted to. He was determined to go through with it.

"Yeah," he replied, "I got interested in what you said the other night. What is it with that religion of yours?"

Bill was momentarily overwhelmed. *This is more than I hoped for – Hank's asking me to tell him what I've wanted to tell him.* "I was hoping that's what you wanted to talk about. It isn't religion, Hank. Not, really. It's a whole new way of life. And I can tell you right now that it's the greatest thing that ever happened to me."

The Warren boy licked his lips in an effort to get rid of the hot, dry feeling in his mouth. Bill talked the same way Letitia did. He had tried to ignore what his sister said, but now Bill Anderson was repeating her words. He was as happy as Letitia was.

"I don't know whether I buy that religious bit," he continued, ignoring Bill's protest that he wasn't religious. "And I sure don't want to be an oddball about it." He turned on a side road and slowed to a crawl. "I was going to talk to my sister. I wanted to get the answers to some questions. But she gets so pushy about it I decided not to. If I say anything to her, she'd think she was going to convert me." His voice rose. "And I'm not having any part of it!"

"I know how you feel," Bill replied. "I think I would have been the same way myself. It all looks so strange from the outside. A guy gets afraid that becoming a Christian means you have to do a lot of weird things you don't want to do. But I've never done anything offbeat since I've become a Christian. I feel like I've just been myself. Maybe I've even been more myself than ever before. So I'm a different person from Letitia or from the Davis triplets. That means I'll do different things. So Letitia gets a kick out of singing worship songs all over the place. Well, that's her. Me, I'm the quiet type. I can't even pray in front of a group like Doug or Del can. But I happen to think that God respects my personality and won't force me into these things until I'm ready. I know what you're afraid of, Hank. You're afraid that if you become a Christian, you'll have to do every funny little thing every other Christian does. But that's not the case."

Bill paused, surprised by his own speech. He never knew he could speak so strongly and accurately. It wasn't easy for him to put ideas and insights into words. Not ordinarily. *Thank You, God,* he said silently.

Hank sat waiting for Bill to go on. He had stopped the car next to a farm field.

Bill continued, "You know, a guy needs somebody to guide him through life. Our parents can't always help us, and they don't know all the answers anyway. I want somebody to help me figure out how to live – somebody I can really trust. I guess I finally realized that I was messing up my own life pretty badly and I needed somebody to pull me back on my feet and get me going in the right direction. You've known me for four years, Hank. You saw what kind of life I was living until recently."

Hank nodded. Bill had run with a wild bunch. They had never gone into drugs, but he didn't suppose that was because they had convictions against it. They had more than their share of beer parties, and there was a rumor that they were the ones who had ransacked several small country churches a year earlier. No decent girls would go out with any of them.

Yes, Bill had been getting a good start at wasting his life.

"Nobody had to tell me I wasn't living the way

I should," Bill went on. "I already knew that. But I didn't realize the consequences of what I was doing. I was ruining my soul."

Hank reached down and turned off the ignition. The cold white moonlight flooded down on the field and into the windows.

"Your sister talked to me one day, Hank. She explained to me that all the bad things I'd done had put a real big barrier between me and God. He's so good and holy and perfect that I'd never get through to Him in my condition."

Hank cleared his throat. "So where did you go from there?"

"That's where Jesus Christ comes in. He's the one guy who's lived a perfectly good life. God sent Him to do that. So because He lived a sinless life, He was able to offer Himself to take my place in getting the punishment I deserved. He got it instead. So now I can come to God and say, 'Look, I know I did bad things and I'm sorry. Thanks for sending Jesus.' I know I can go to God my Father and not get zapped."

Hank stared out over the stubble of old, dried cornstalks. "But I haven't done the things you have, Bill. I really don't feel I've messed up my life. I've kept off the drug scene, steered clear of drinking, worked hard in school, and listened to my parents." He paused, remembering the sharp comment to his mother that evening as he walked out the door. "Well, usually I'm pretty respectful to my parents.

Bill, I really feel like I can run my own life. I plan to go to college, get married and have a family, and be a good citizen. So what do I need religion for?"

"It's true you're not a bad guy." Bill had always respected Hank, a guy who could be good and manly at the same time. "But you must think you need something, or you wouldn't have gotten me out here."

Hank laughed nervously. "Yeah, you're right. So why am I out here talking about all this with you? I guess because I can't sleep at nights and don't even know why."

"Well, maybe God's trying to get through to you, Hank. Have you been feeling lately like maybe your own goodness isn't quite good enough?"

Hank smiled sheepishly and said nothing.

"And maybe Letitia's getting through, too," continued Bill thoughtfully. "She's got a fantastic outlook on life now. She's so happy and outgoing and cares about everybody. I bet you can't help but see the change in her life." He looked at Hank closely. "I bet all her happiness really looks good to you."

Hank stared down at the gas pedal. Bill was really hitting the nail on the head. *The guy's really reading me,* he said to himself.

They sat silent for a while, Hank struggling with his thoughts. Bill glanced at him occasionally, wondering what to say next.

Finally Bill broke the silence. "It's a whole new life that God can give you, Hank. Be great if you started now."

Hank said nothing.

Bill looked out over the cornfield and shivered slightly. He hadn't noticed the chill until now. *Sure hope I haven't said anything wrong. He's been thinking about this stuff pretty hard for months, I bet.* He glanced down at his wrist without moving his hand. *Ten o'clock already. Really shoots my history test tomorrow.*

Hank cleared his throat. "Bill, how do I go about getting this new life?"

Bill smiled. "I'll tell you. It's as easy as asking."

* * *

The following morning Hank met Del in the corridor near his locker. "I've got to tell you what happened to me last night."

Del studied his face. "Whatever it was, it must have been good."

"You can say that again. I've got the same new life that you guys and Bill and Letitia have."

Del stared at him. "That's terrific. Does Letitia know?"

"I told her last night after Bill and I did some serious talking about it and I decided that I had to have a personal relationship with Jesus." Quickly he related what had happened. "I've been thinking about it quite a while. A couple of times I tried to talk to you, but it didn't work out."

Del thought a moment. "Oh, like that day at the Hitching Post."

"Yeah."

They left the row of lockers and moved in the direction of their homerooms. "I figured you were a Christian or Letitia wouldn't be dating you."

Del wanted him to keep talking, but Bill approached just then and Hank hurried over to him. "I'll see you around, Del."

"Hi, Del," said Bill, smiling. "Guess you heard the good news."

The Davis boy watched as Bill and Hank walked down the wide hall together. It was tremendous that Letitia's brother was a believer now, but Del was deeply disturbed by some of the things Hank said. He hadn't spelled it out, but he hadn't been sure Del was a believer. But he had known Bill was a Christian. His faith was only a few weeks old, but half the guys in school knew about it.

Del went uneasily to his homeroom, wondering how many others he had missed the opportunity of talking to about Jesus Christ because he kept so quiet they hadn't known where he really stood. All day he was upset by it.

He could have had the joy of leading Hank to Christ. Letitia's brother had even tried to approach him, but he hadn't responded. Now that joy had gone to someone else! He sat down and leafed through his history book.

* * *

Letitia and Del sat in the Warren's family room. Del drained the last few drops of cream soda from his glass. Letitia ignored her own full glass of cola.

"Del, you can't beat yourself for what happened. Do you think the Christian life is like a football game? We're not competing with each other to see who can be the best soul winner. You almost seem to feel that Bill has beaten you out of some kind of position."

"No," protested Del. "It's not that."

"Yes, it is," insisted Letitia. "I can see it very plainly. I haven't lived for years with a brother without picking up a few facts about the male ego. You feel like you missed out on the joy of leading Hank to Christ. But maybe God wanted Bill to have that joy. Maybe God on purpose kept that conversation in the Hitching Post from continuing."

"I never thought of that," mused Del.

"Maybe," said Letitia, "I should be the one to feel bad. I've pestered Hank for months and really done things that embarrassed him. He's really been sore at me, and I don't blame him."

She paused and sipped from her glass. "Maybe you think I was deliriously happy when I found out about Hank. Well, I was happy – but do you know what, Del? I was jealous, too, because the Lord hadn't used *me* to be His instrument in leading Hank to Jesus. I'm really ashamed of myself."

Her delicate face looked tired suddenly. She stopped talking and drank her cola quietly. Del chewed on an ice cube and looked at her with new understanding.

"We sure haven't thought about Bill, have we?" he said finally. "Bill's just a new Christian. He's led a rough life, and his old friends have given him the cold shoulder. What better encouragement for him than to get to lead Hank to Jesus? Now he and Hank will be good friends. Bill needs a good buddy. And the two of them can grow together in the Christian life. I never thought about that."

Del smiled at Letitia. "Does it ever seem to you like God does really neat things? And sometimes we almost don't even notice them."